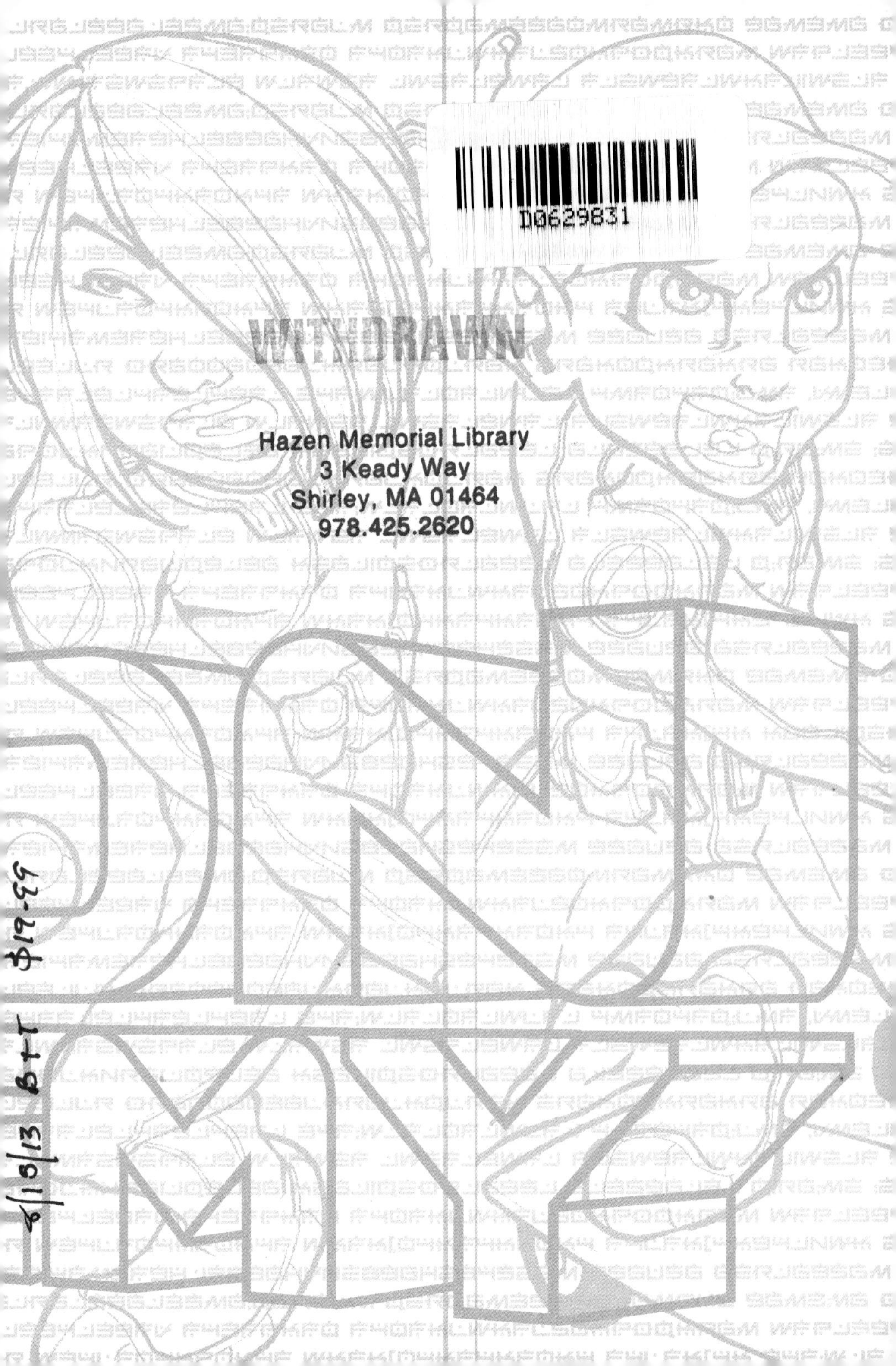

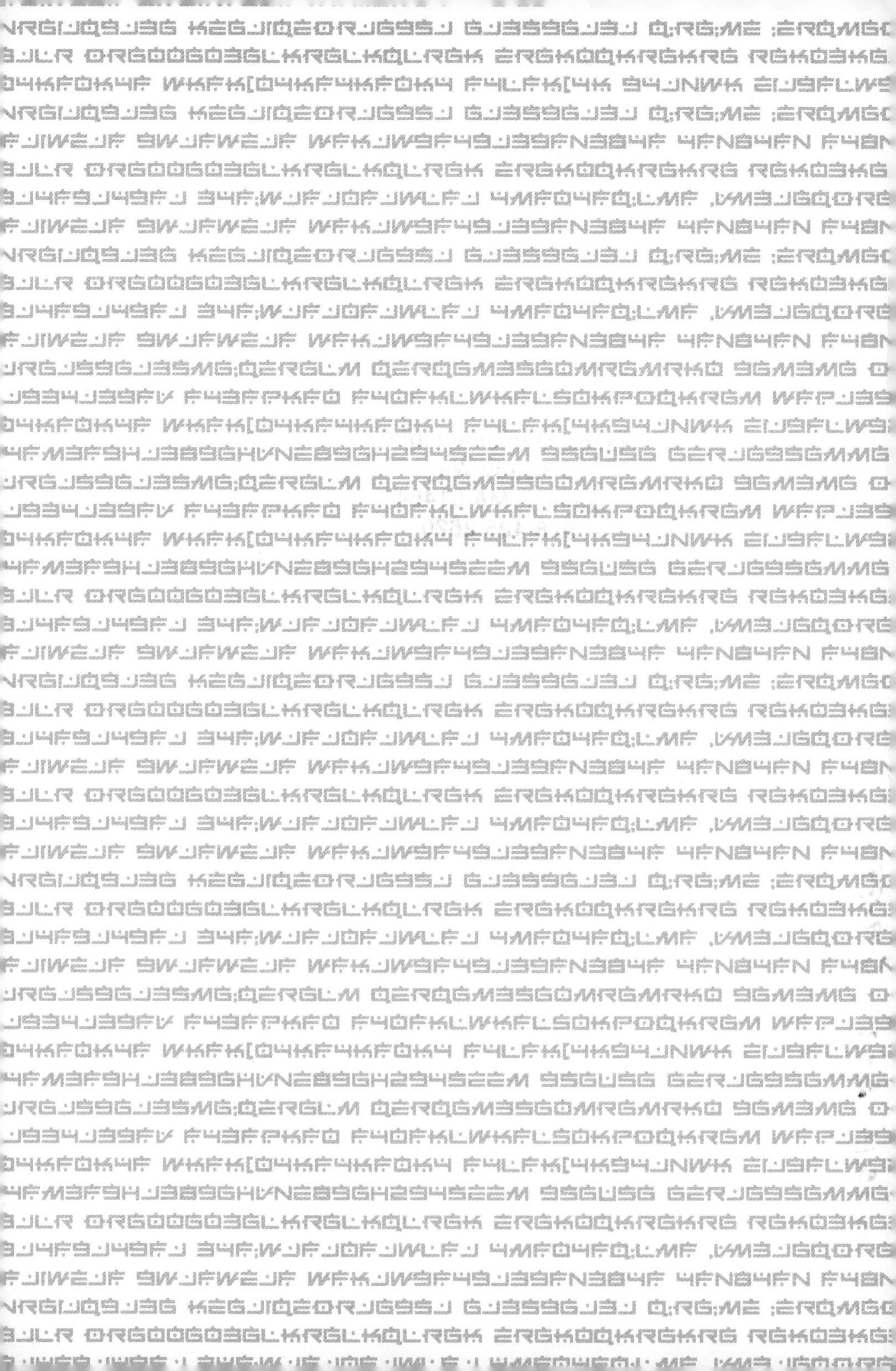

RECON ACADEMY

STORM SURGE

FILE NO. 1437578

BY CHRIS EVERHEART
ILLUSTRATED BY ARCANA STUDIO

ACCESS GRANTED ⟩⟩⟩⟩

STONE ARCH BOOKS
MINNEAPOLIS   SAN DIEGO

Recon Academy is published by Stone Arch Books
A Capstone Imprint
151 Good Counsel Drive, P.O. Box 669
Mankato, Minnesota 56002
www.capstonepub.com

Cataloging-in-Publication Data is available on the Library of Congress
website.

Library binding: 978-1-4342-1918-3

Summary: Emmi, Jay, and Ryker are rock-climbing in the mountains
when a storm hits, ruining their field trip. As they descend Seaside Peak,
Hazmat radios from base, delivering some bad news — national security
is at risk! A Navy submarine is unable to upload top-secret data because
the storm has knocked down the antenna on Seaside Peak. With the
window of opportunity for the transmission running out, team Recon will
have to find a way to get to the antenna soon!

Designer: Brann Garvey
Art Director: Bob Lentz
Production Specialist: Michelle Biedscheid
Series Editor: Donnie Lemke
Series Concept: Michael Dahl, Brann Garvey, Heather Kindseth,
    Donnie Lemke

Printed in the United States of America in Stevens Point, Wisconsin.
092009
005619WZS10

› TABLE OF CONTENTS

››››
ENTER

 › GADGETRY

 › MARTIAL ARTS

 › COMPUTERS

 › FORENSICS

TEAM BREAKDOWN

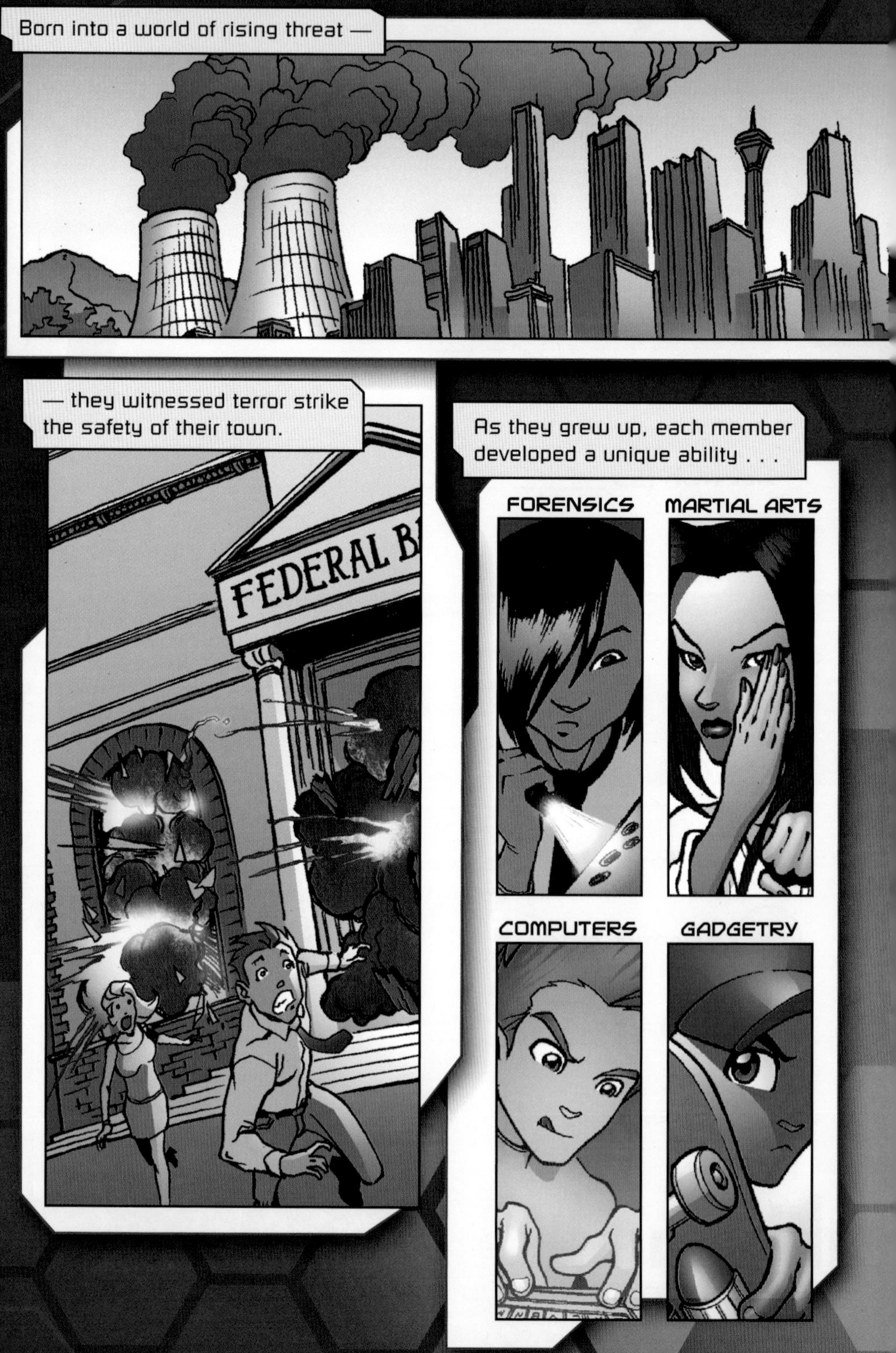
Born into a world of rising threat —
— they witnessed terror strike the safety of their town.
FEDERAL B
As they grew up, each member developed a unique ability . . .
FORENSICS
MARTIAL ARTS
COMPUTERS
GADGETRY

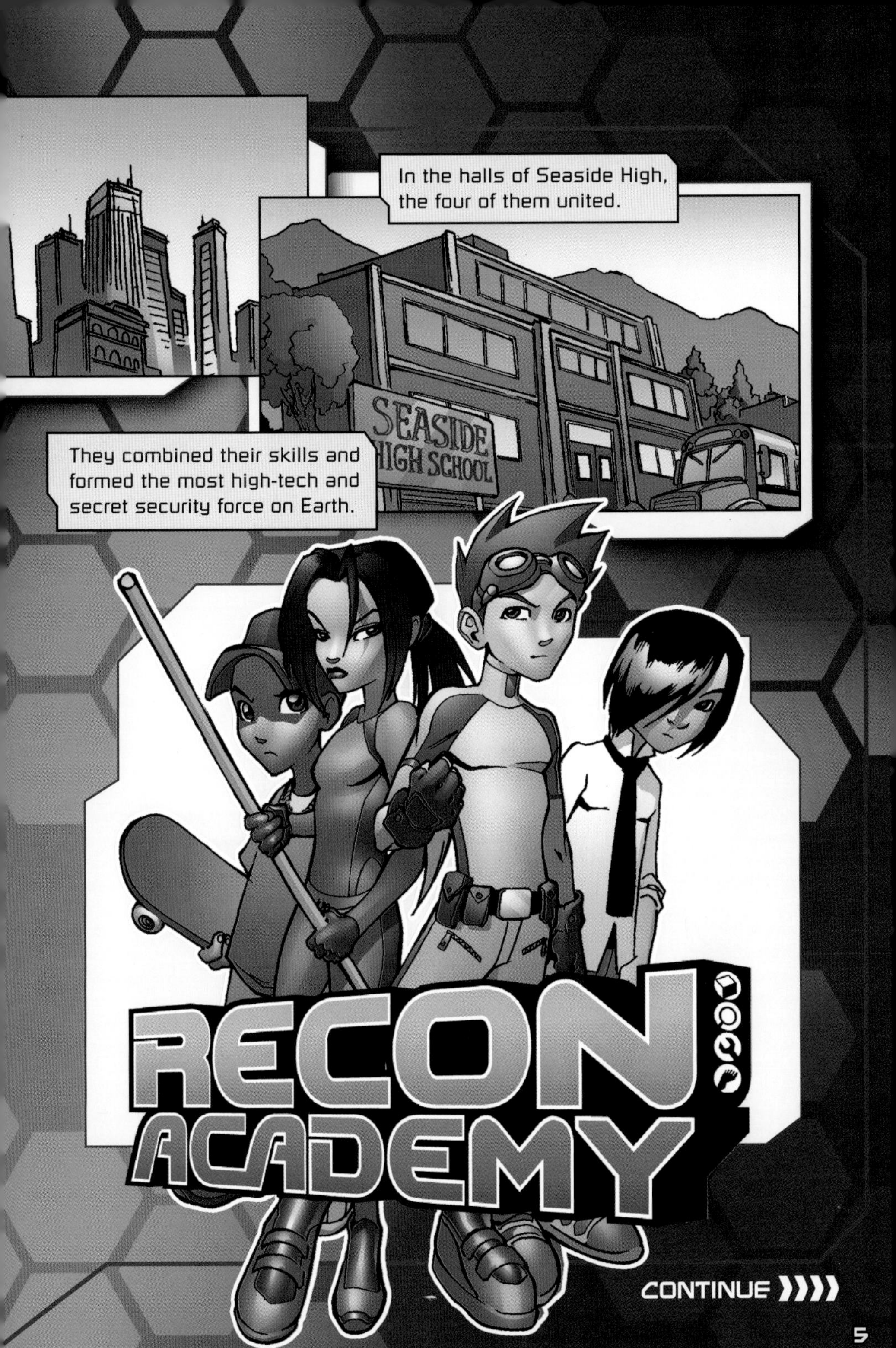
In the halls of Seaside High, the four of them united.
SEASIDE HIGH SCHOOL
They combined their skills and formed the most high-tech and secret security force on Earth.
RECON ACADEMY
CONTINUE

FILE NO. 1437578

SECTION

1

ACCESS GRANTED >>>>

JAY
GADGETRY

128718
293829
9283
98289
89
1
109201
192091
1992

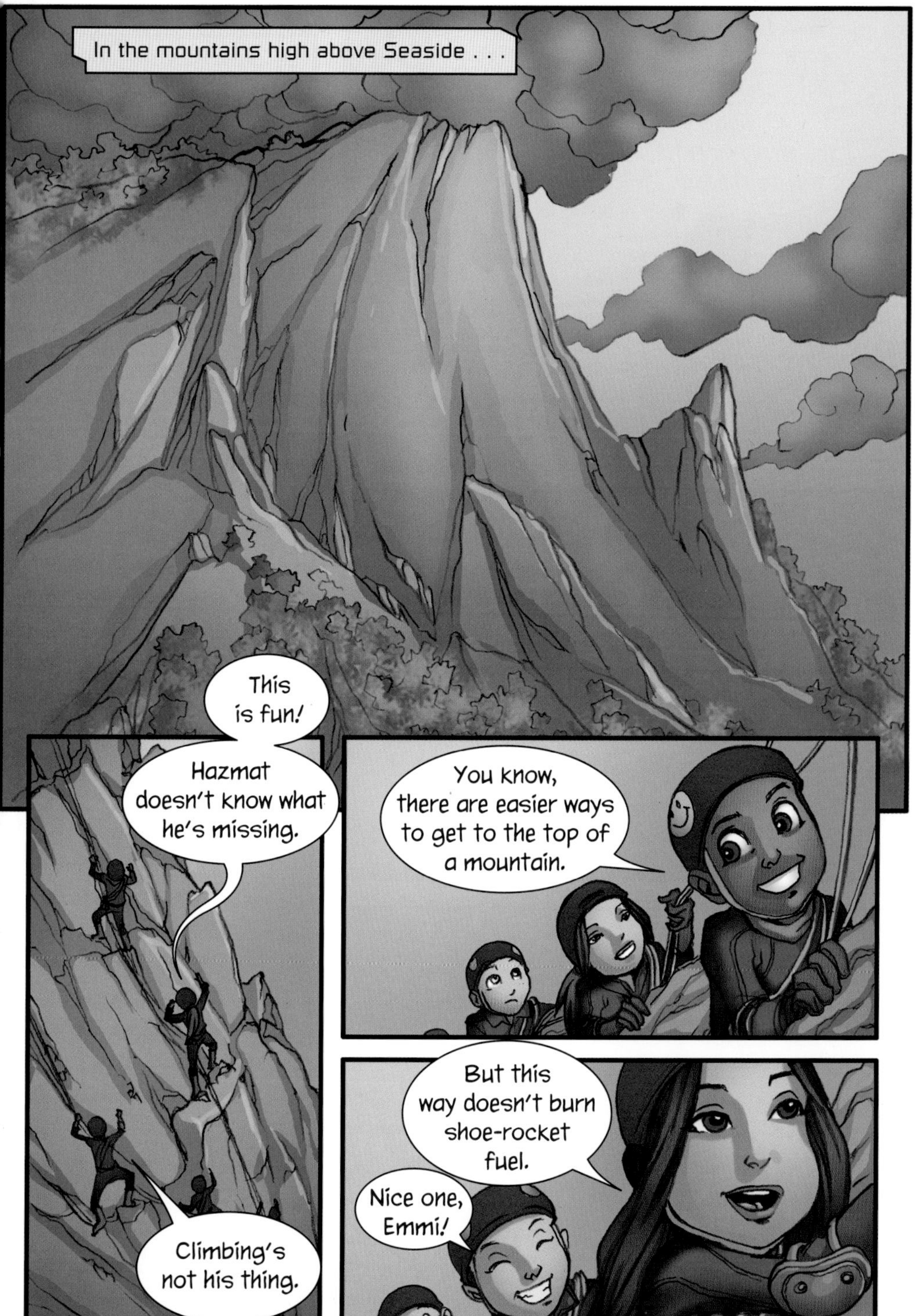
In the mountains high above Seaside . . .
This is fun!
Hazmat doesn't know what he's missing.
Climbing's not his thing.
You know, there are easier ways to get to the top of a mountain.
But this way doesn't burn shoe-rocket fuel.
Nice one, Emmi!

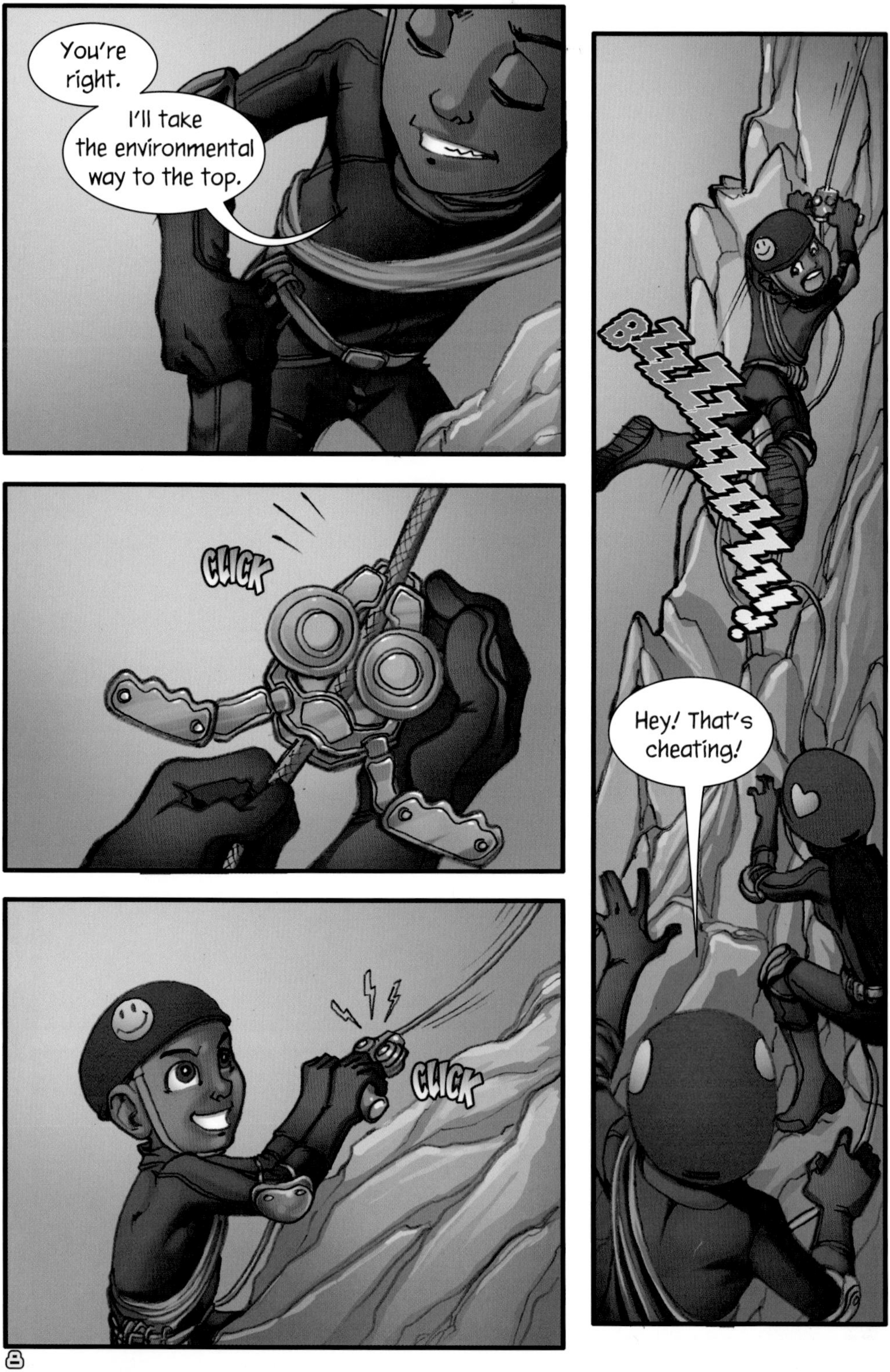

You're right.
I'll take the environmental way to the top.
CLICK
CLICK
BZZZZZZZZZ!!
Hey! That's cheating!

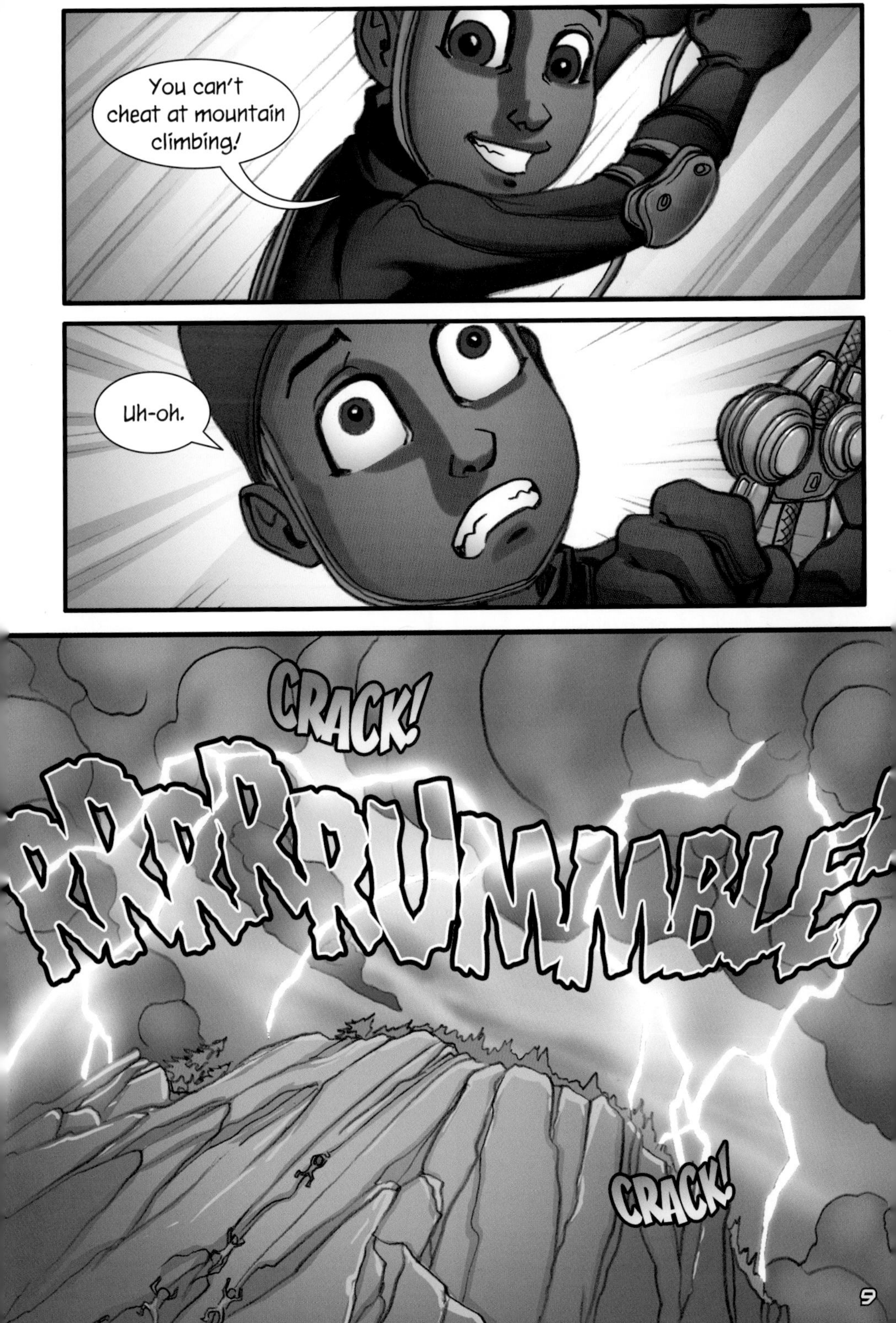
You can't cheat at mountain climbing!
Uh-oh.
CRACK!
RRRRRUMMBLE!
CRACK!

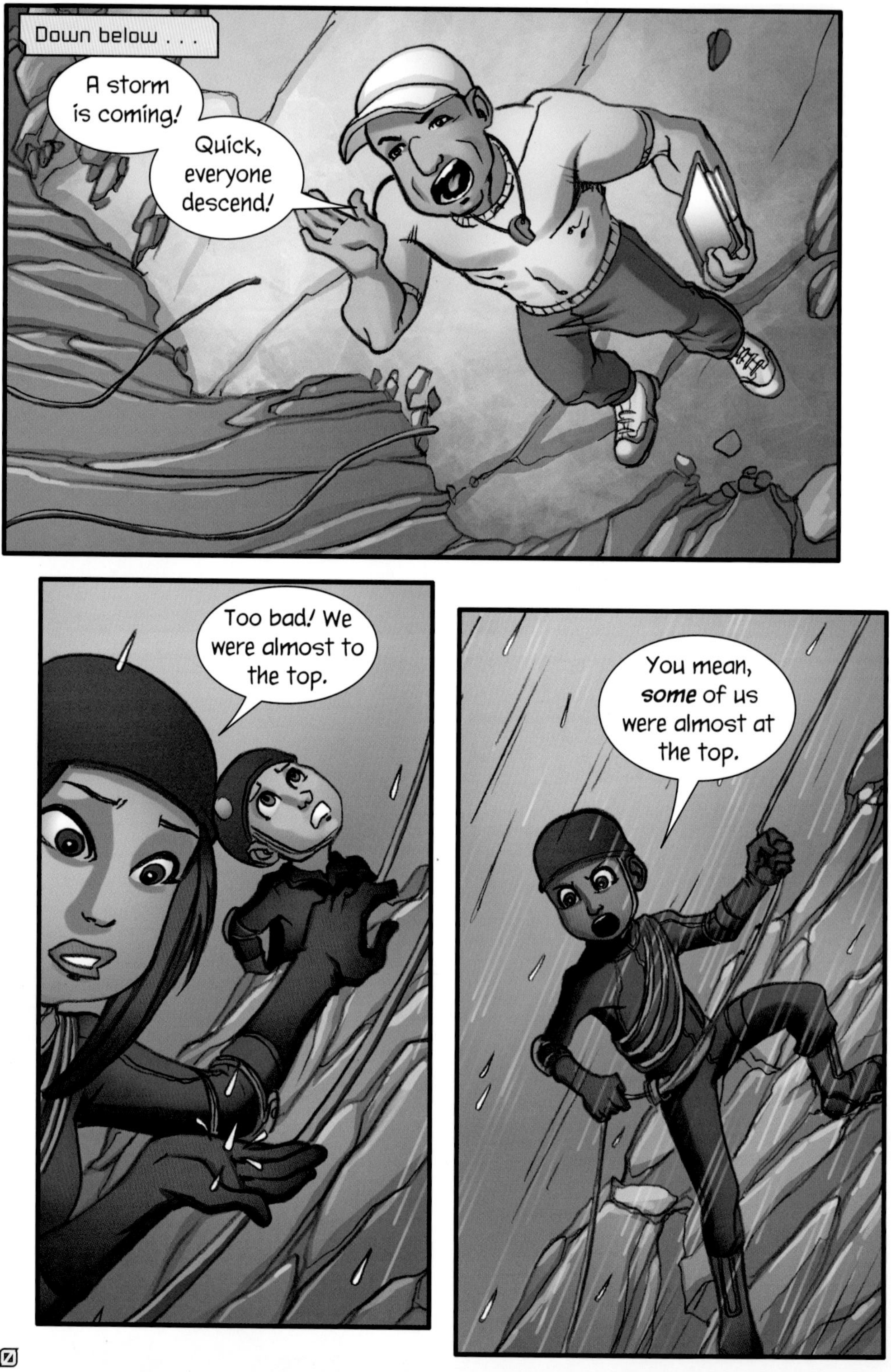
Down below . . .
A storm is coming!
Quick, everyone descend!
Too bad! We were almost to the top.
You mean, *some* of us were almost at the top.

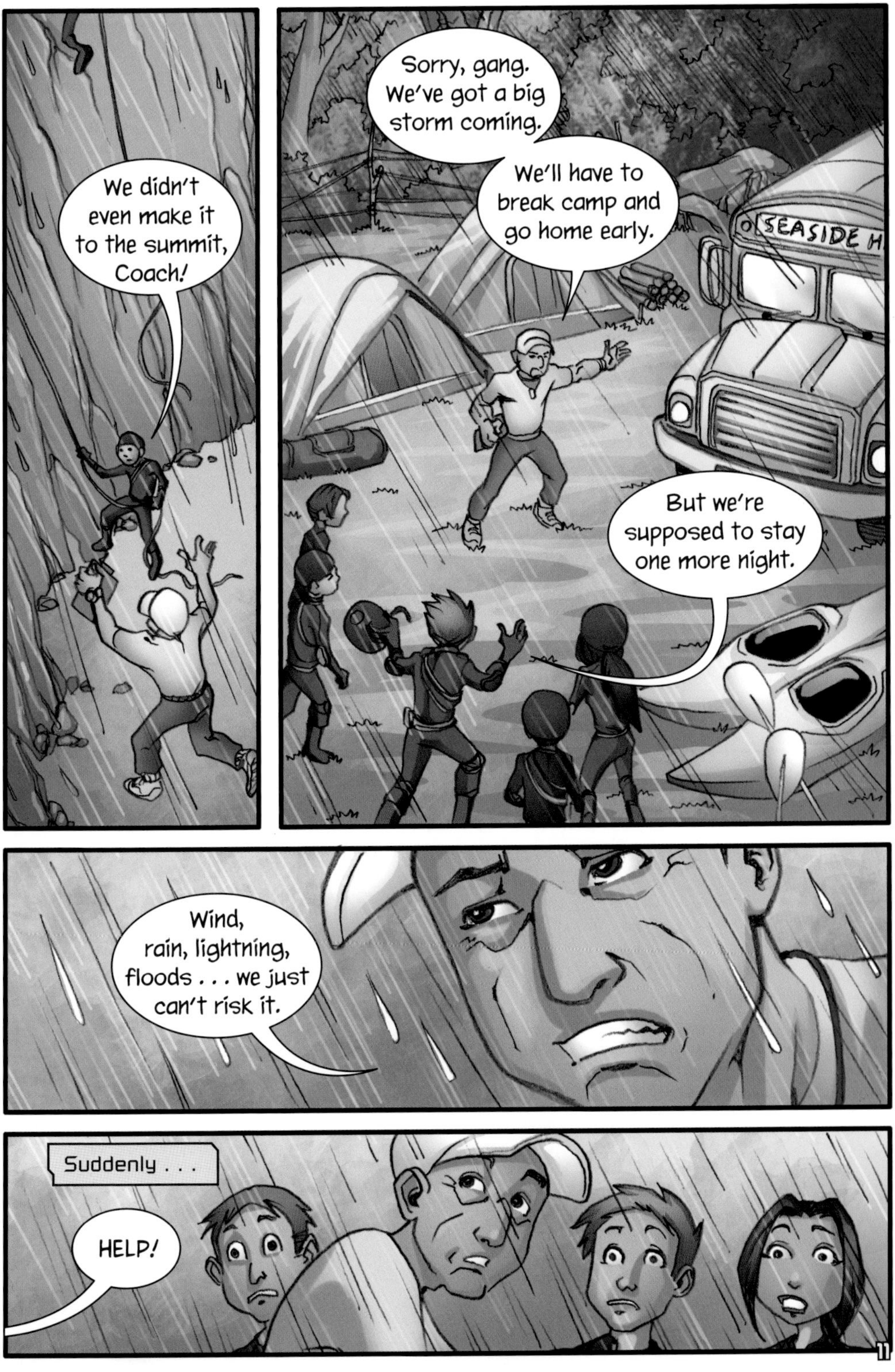
We didn't even make it to the summit, Coach!
Sorry, gang. We've got a big storm coming.
We'll have to break camp and go home early.
But we're supposed to stay one more night.
Wind, rain, lightning, floods . . . we just can't risk it.
Suddenly . . .
HELP!

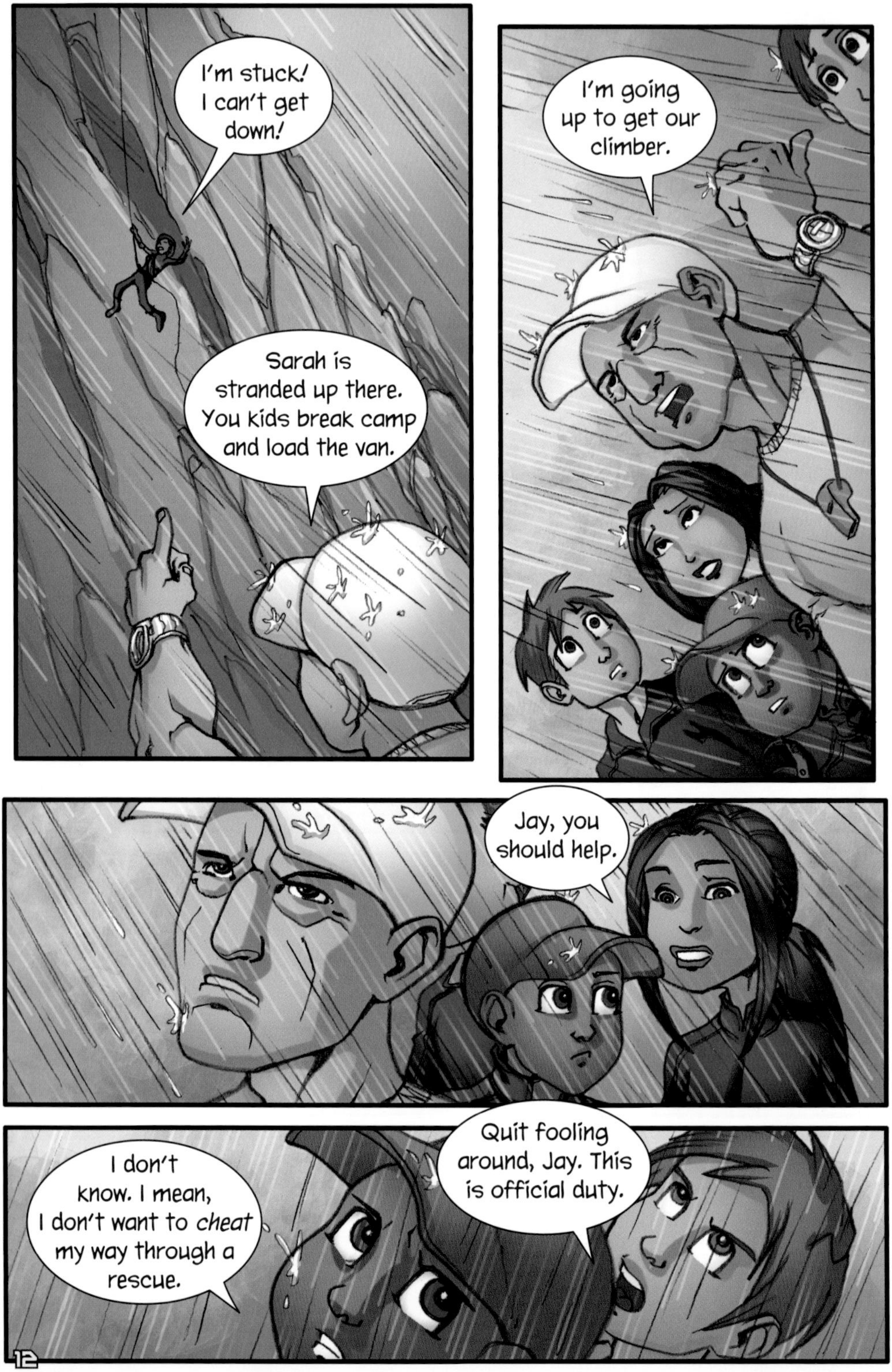
I'm stuck! I can't get down!
Sarah is stranded up there. You kids break camp and load the van.
I'm going up to get our climber.
Jay, you should help.
I don't know. I mean, I don't want to *cheat* my way through a rescue.
Quit fooling around, Jay. This is official duty.

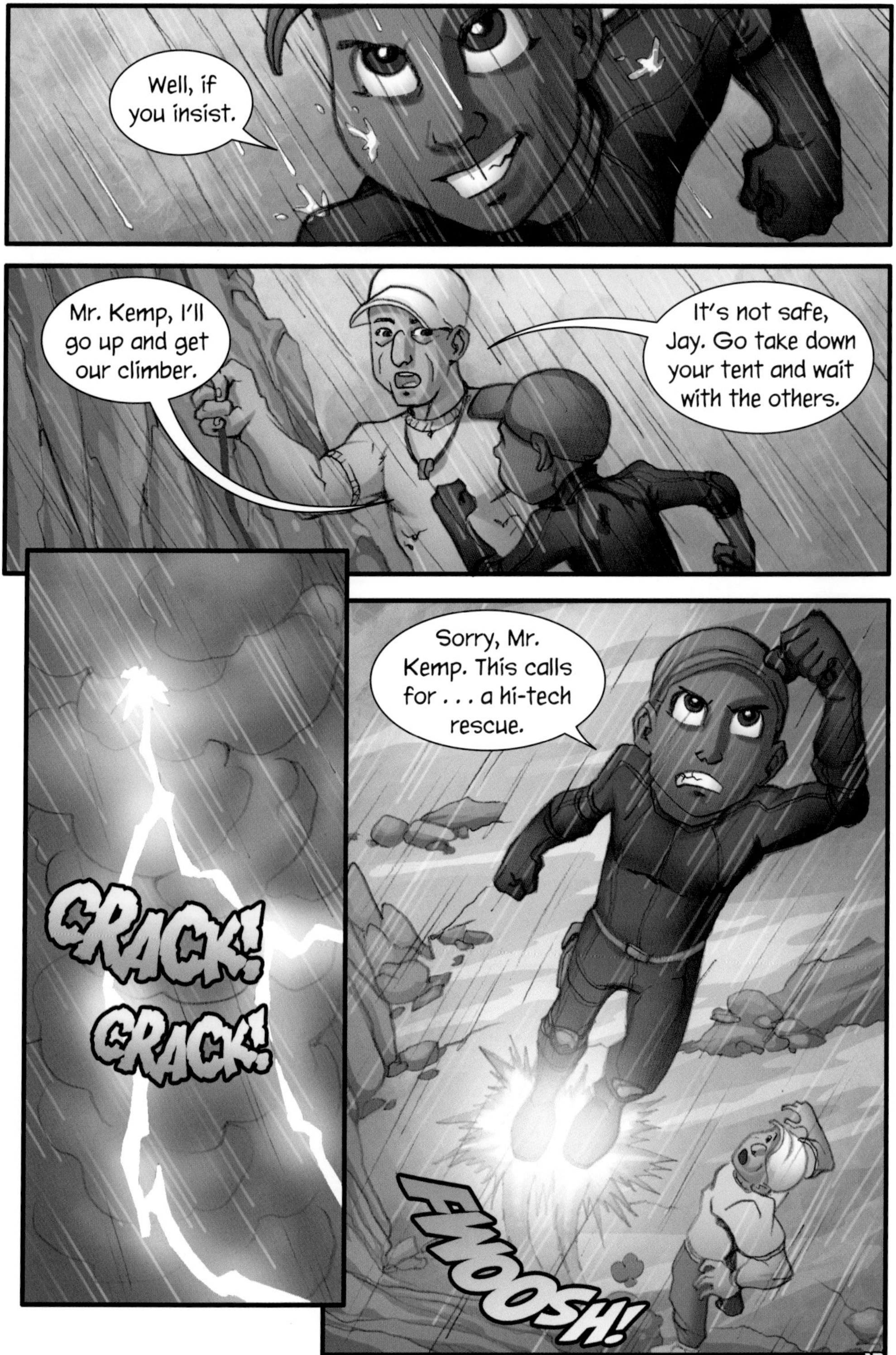
Well, if you insist.
Mr. Kemp, I'll go up and get our climber.
It's not safe, Jay. Go take down your tent and wait with the others.
CRACK! CRACK!
Sorry, Mr. Kemp. This calls for . . . a hi-tech rescue.
FWOOSH!

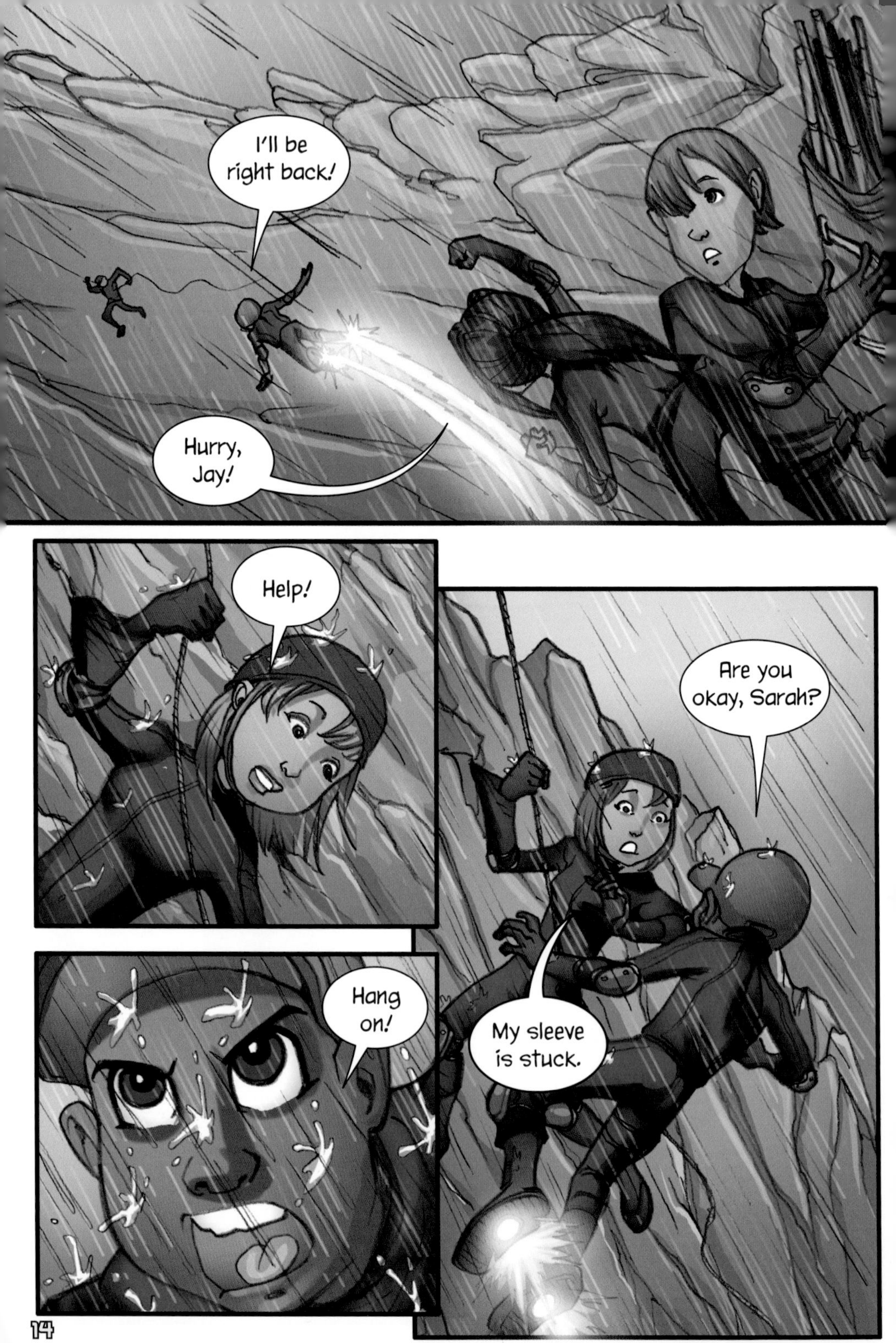
I'll be right back!
Hurry, Jay!
Help!
Are you okay, Sarah?
My sleeve is stuck.
Hang on!

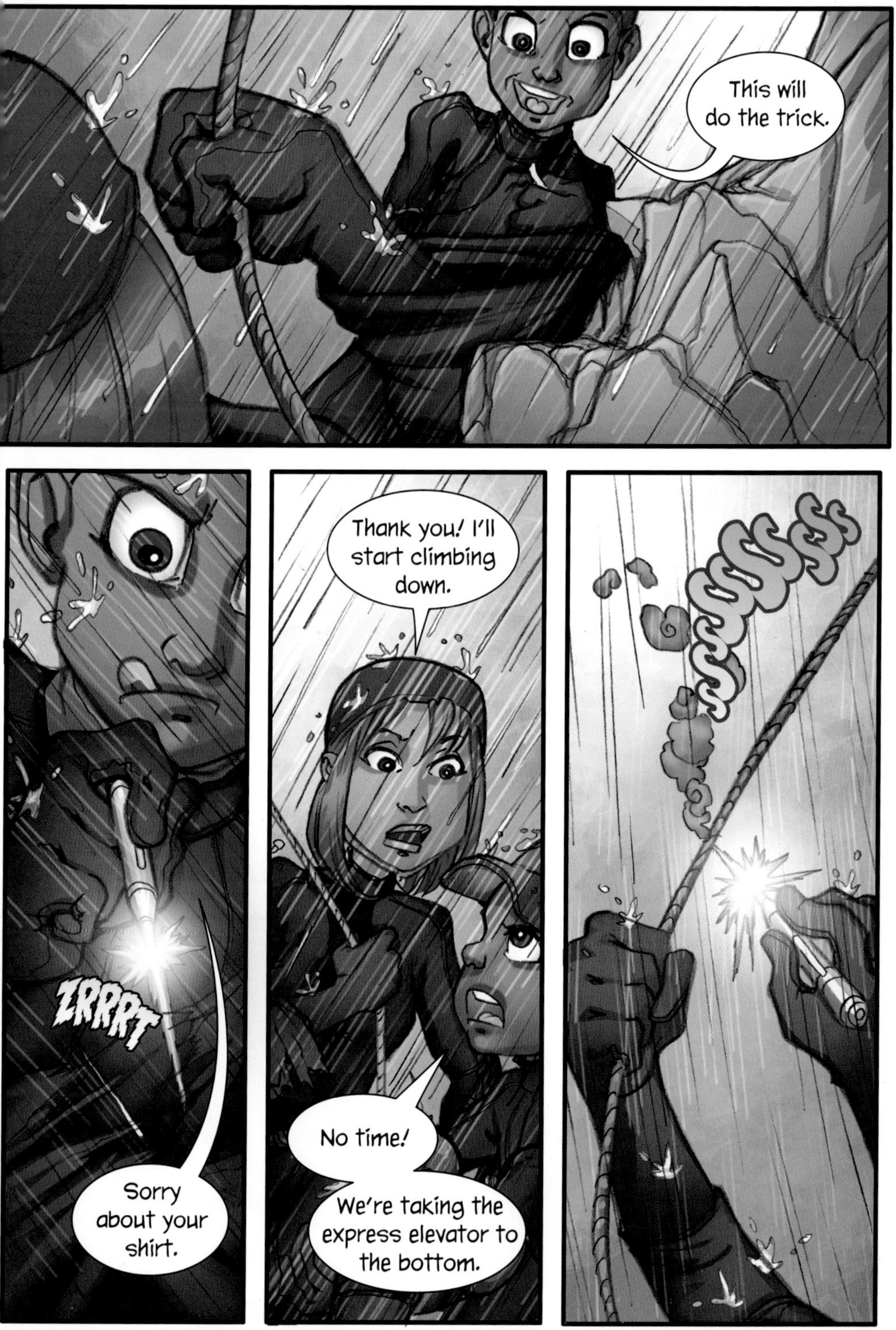
This will do the trick.
ZRRRT
Sorry about your shirt.
Thank you! I'll start climbing down.
No time!
We're taking the express elevator to the bottom.

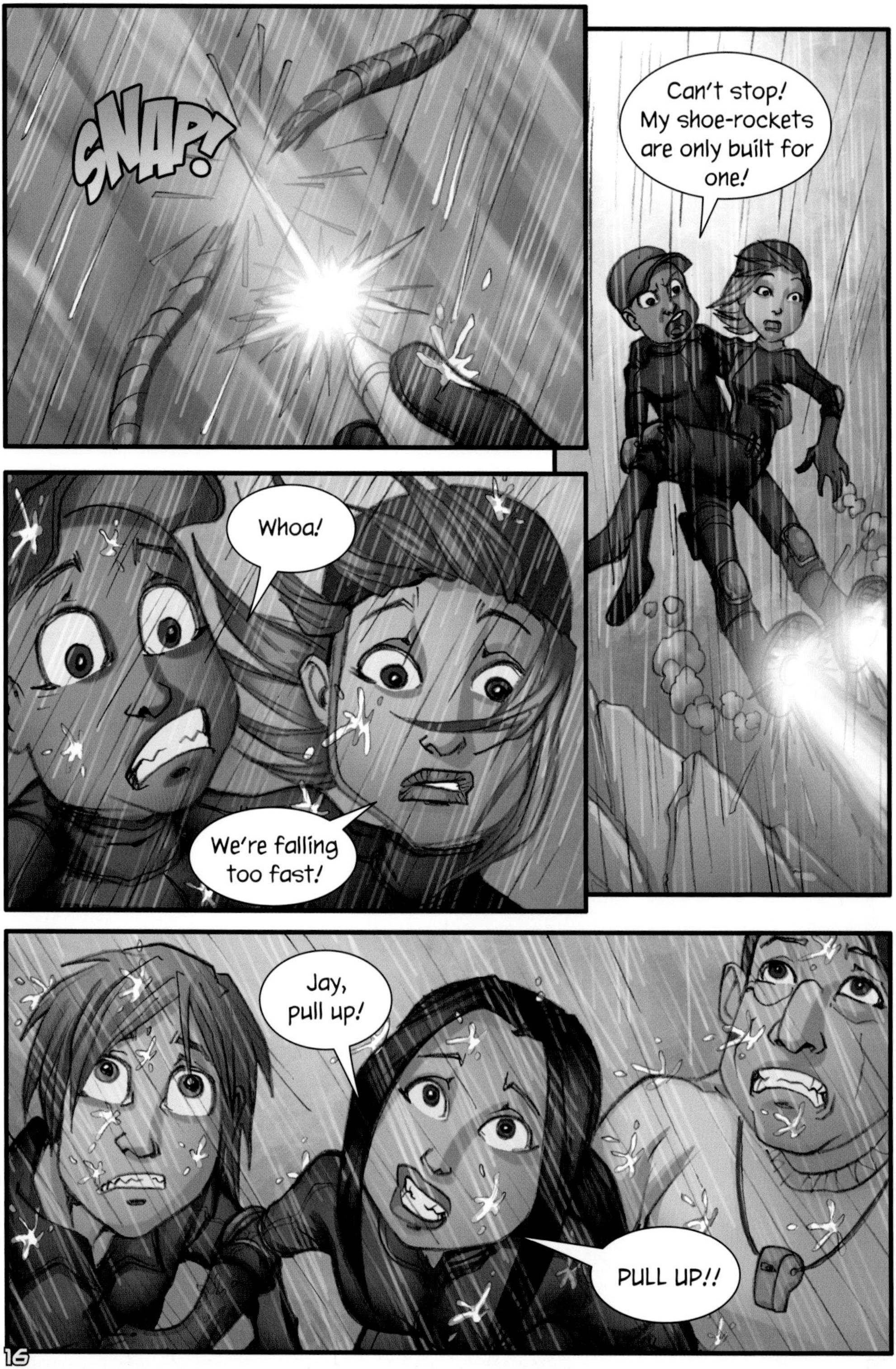
SNAP!
Can't stop! My shoe-rockets are only built for one!
Whoa!
We're falling too fast!
Jay, pull up!
PULL UP!!

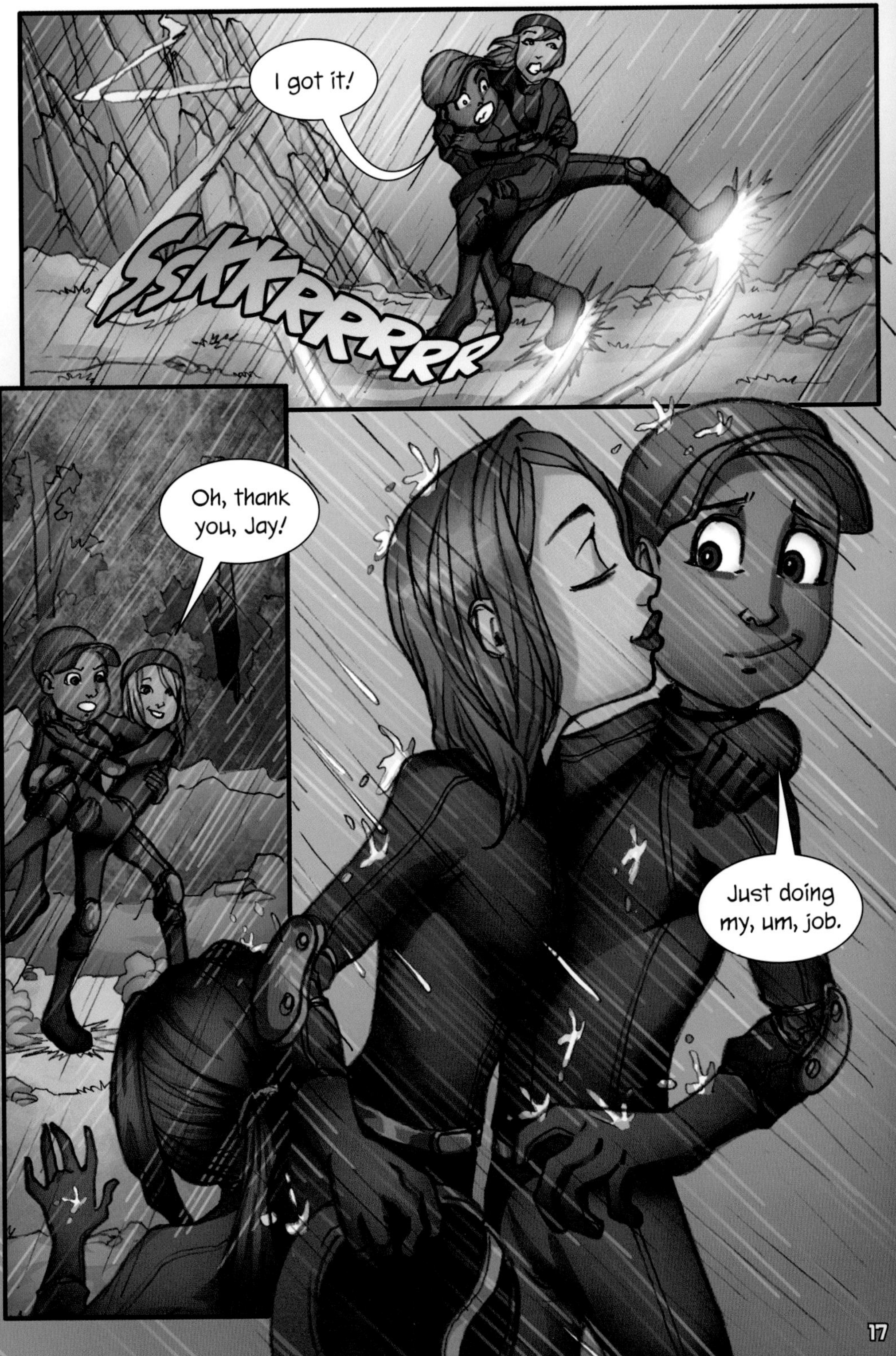
I got it!
SSKKRRRRRR
Oh, thank you, Jay!
Just doing my, um, job.

SECTION

FILE NO.
1437578

2

ACCESS GRANTED ⟩⟩⟩⟩

EMMI
MARTIAL ARTS

128718
293829
9283
98289
89
1
109201
192091
1992

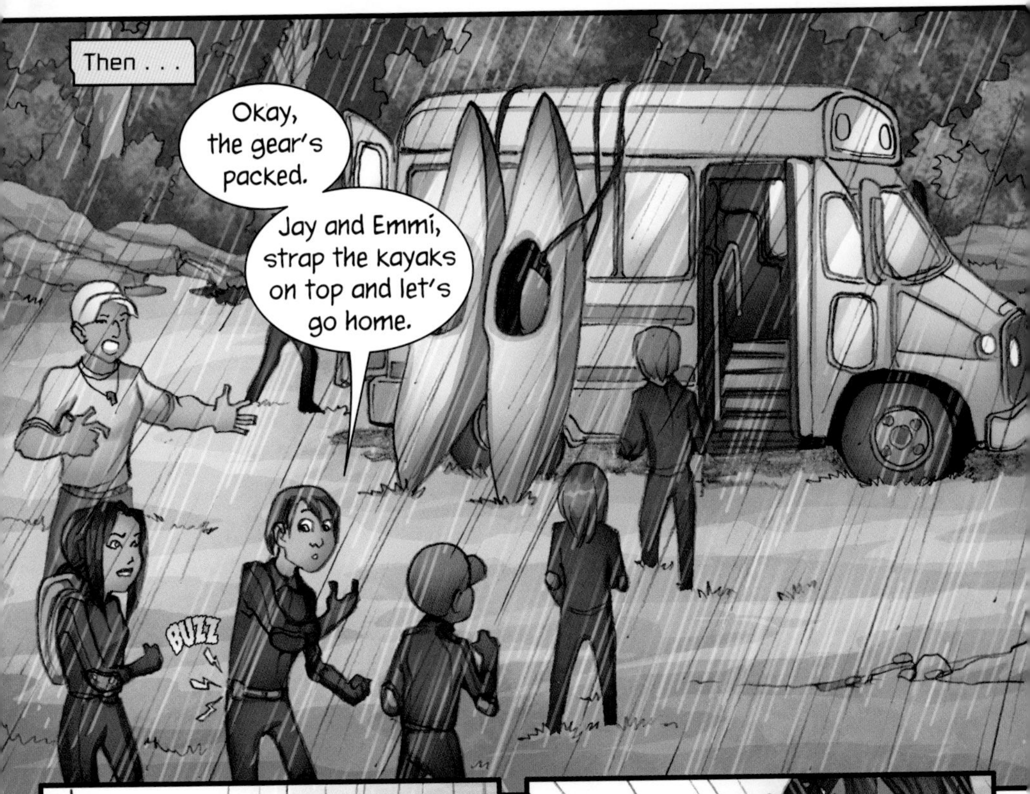
Then . . .
Okay, the gear's packed.
Jay and Emmi, strap the kayaks on top and let's go home.
BUZZ

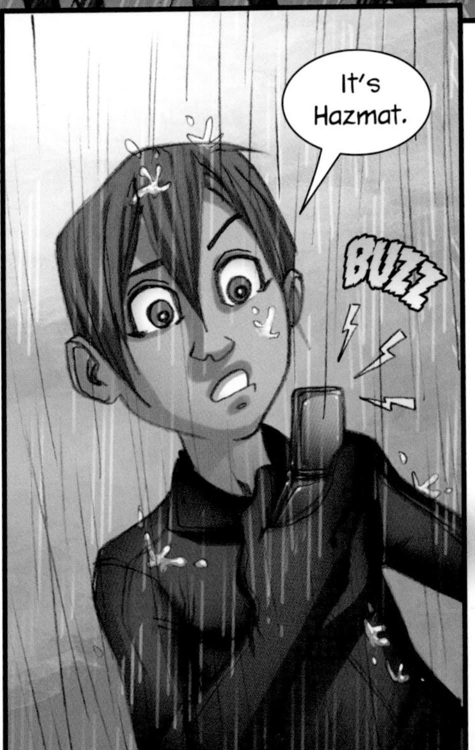
It's Hazmat.
BUZZ

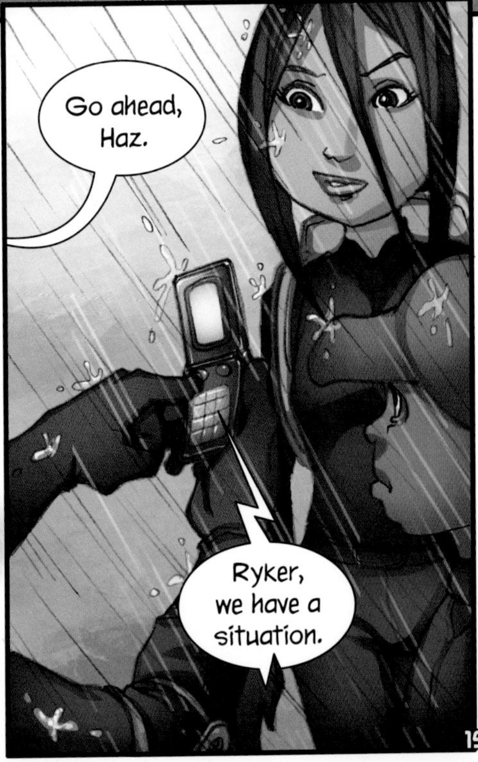
Go ahead, Haz.
Ryker, we have a situation.

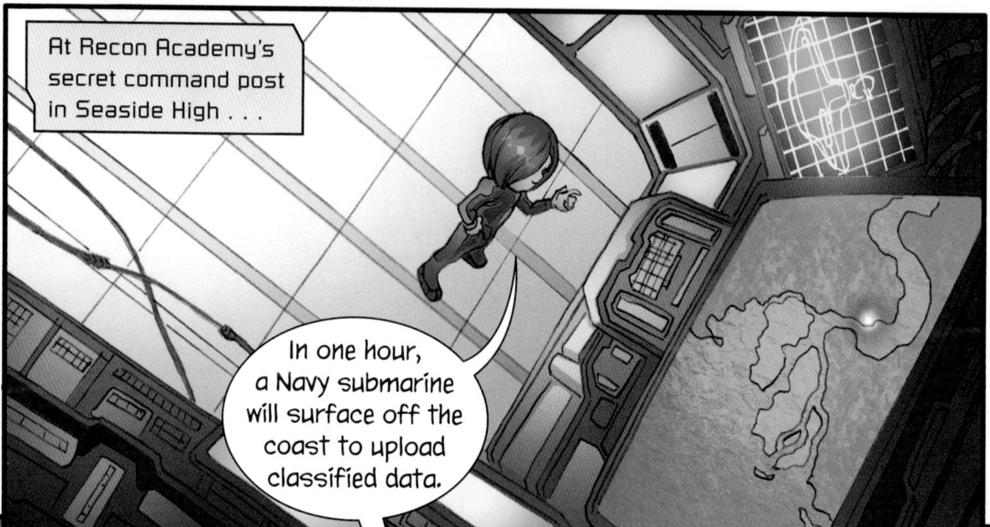
At Recon Academy's secret command post in Seaside High . . .
In one hour, a Navy submarine will surface off the coast to upload classified data.

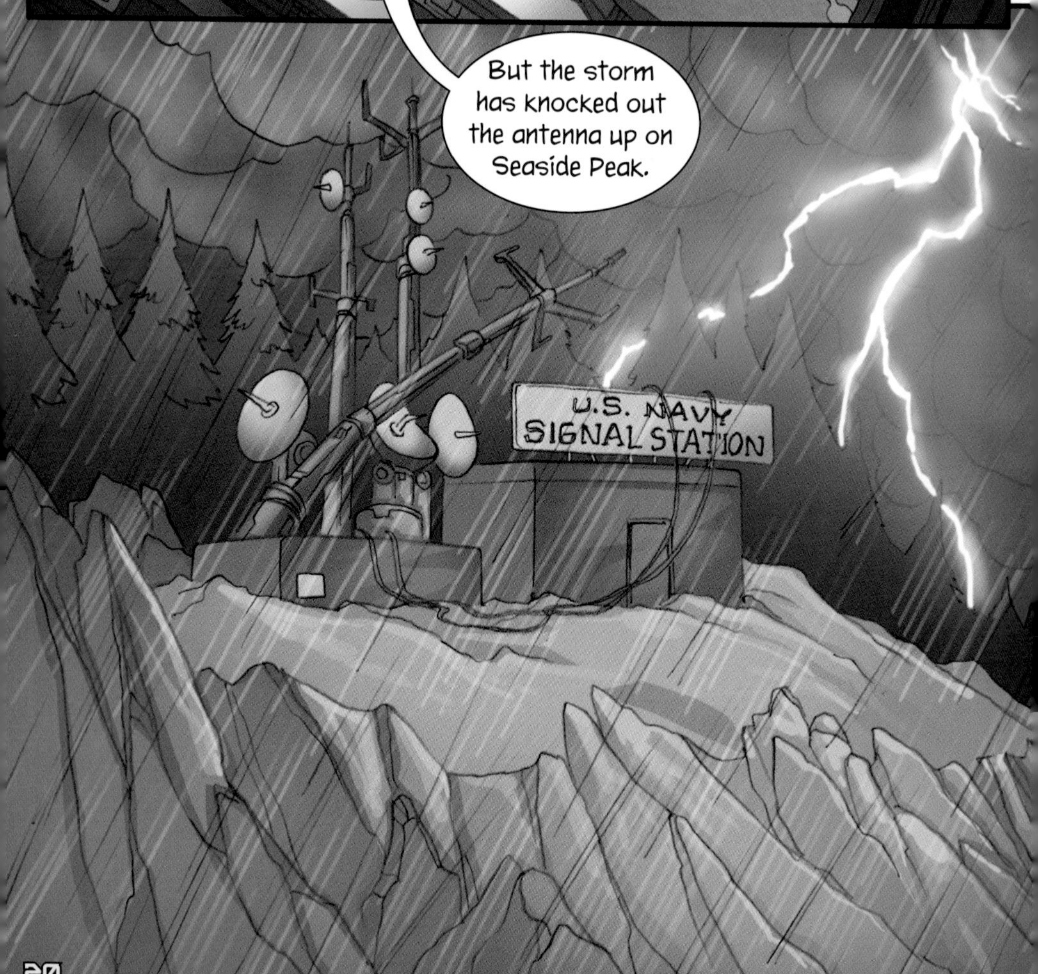
But the storm has knocked out the antenna up on Seaside Peak.
U.S. NAVY SIGNAL STATION

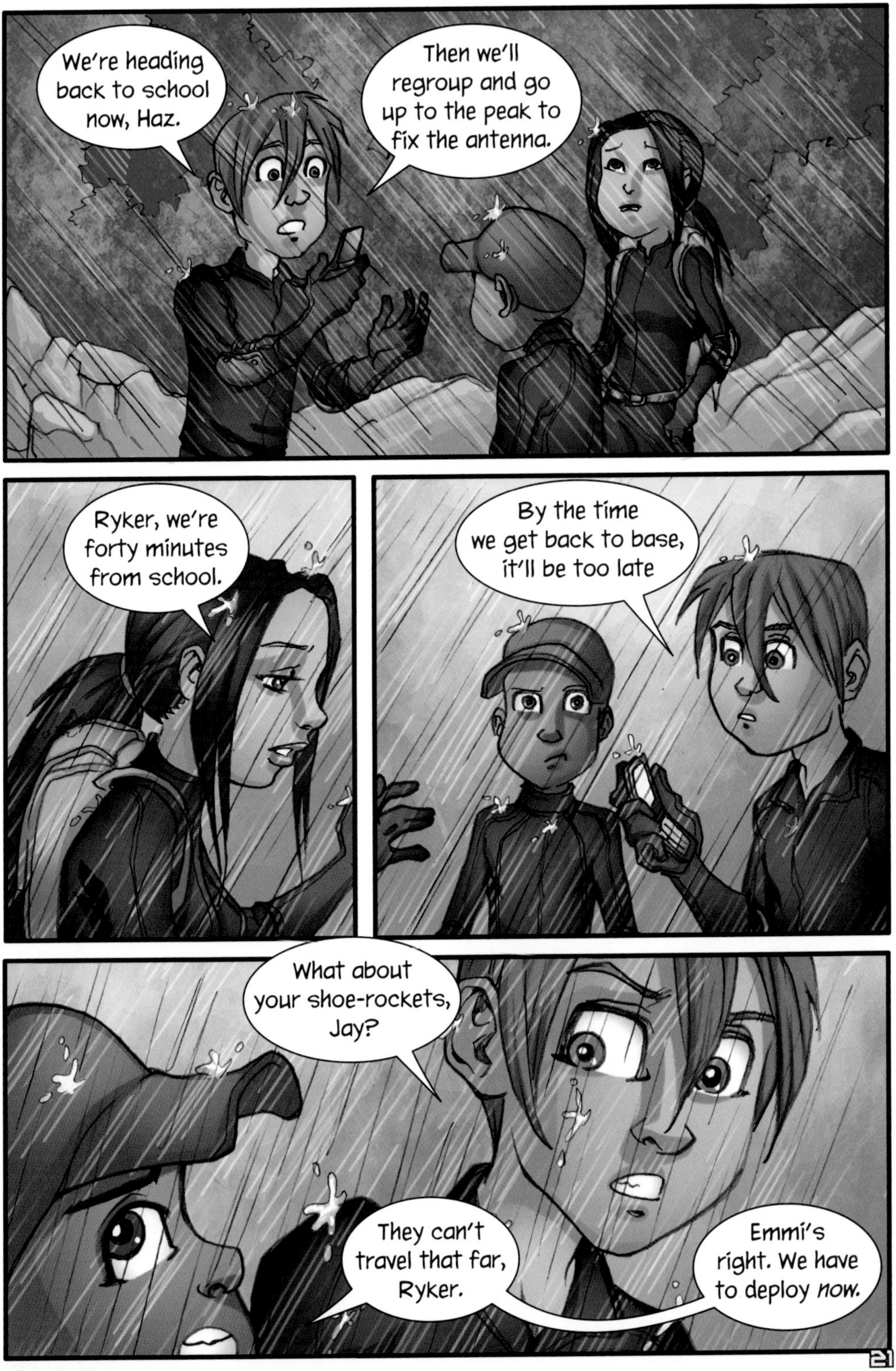
We're heading back to school now, Haz.
Then we'll regroup and go up to the peak to fix the antenna.
Ryker, we're forty minutes from school.
By the time we get back to base, it'll be too late
What about your shoe-rockets, Jay?
They can't travel that far, Ryker.
Emmi's right. We have to deploy *now*.

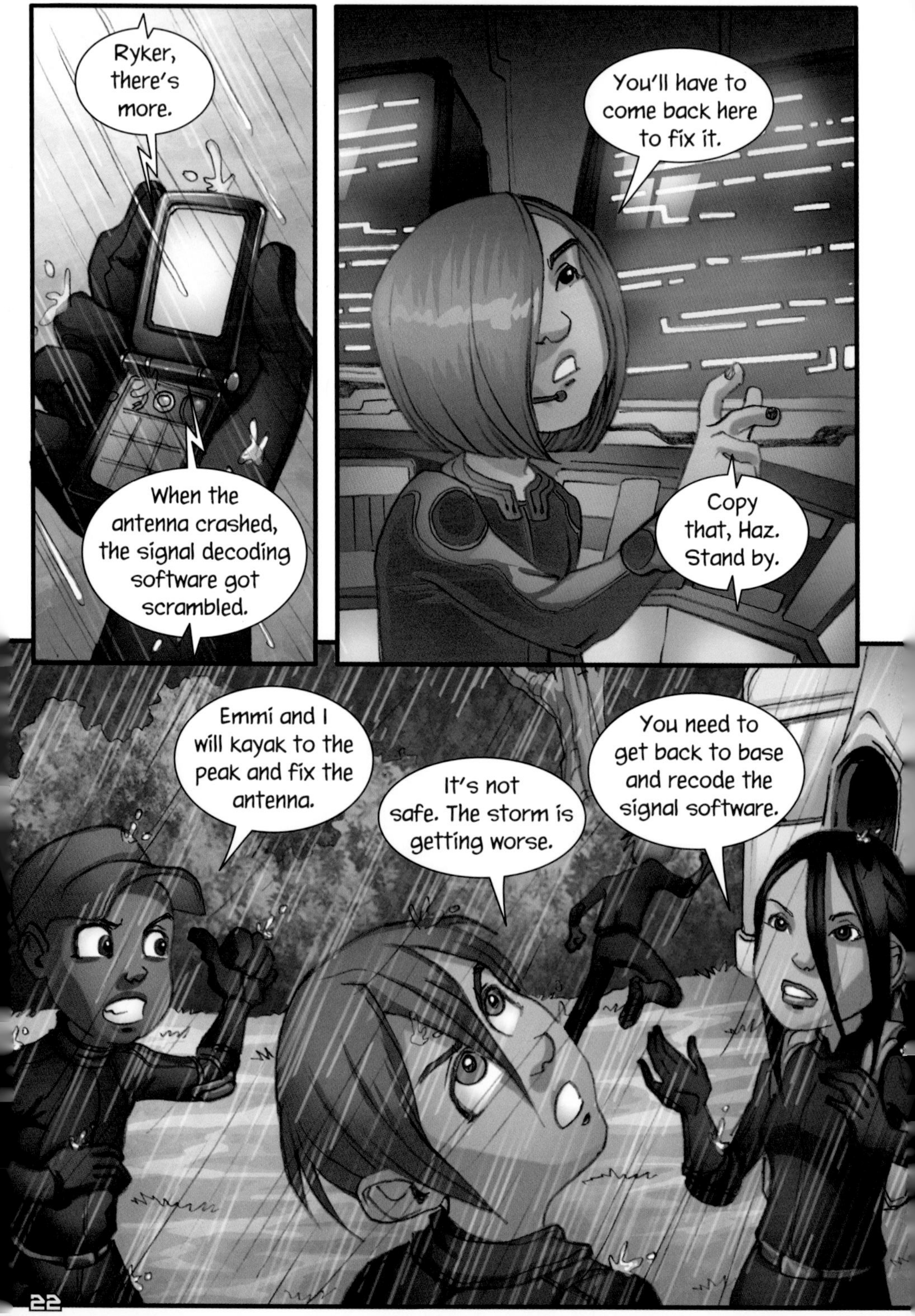
Ryker, there's more.
When the antenna crashed, the signal decoding software got scrambled.
You'll have to come back here to fix it.
Copy that, Haz. Stand by.
Emmi and I will kayak to the peak and fix the antenna.
It's not safe. The storm is getting worse.
You need to get back to base and recode the signal software.

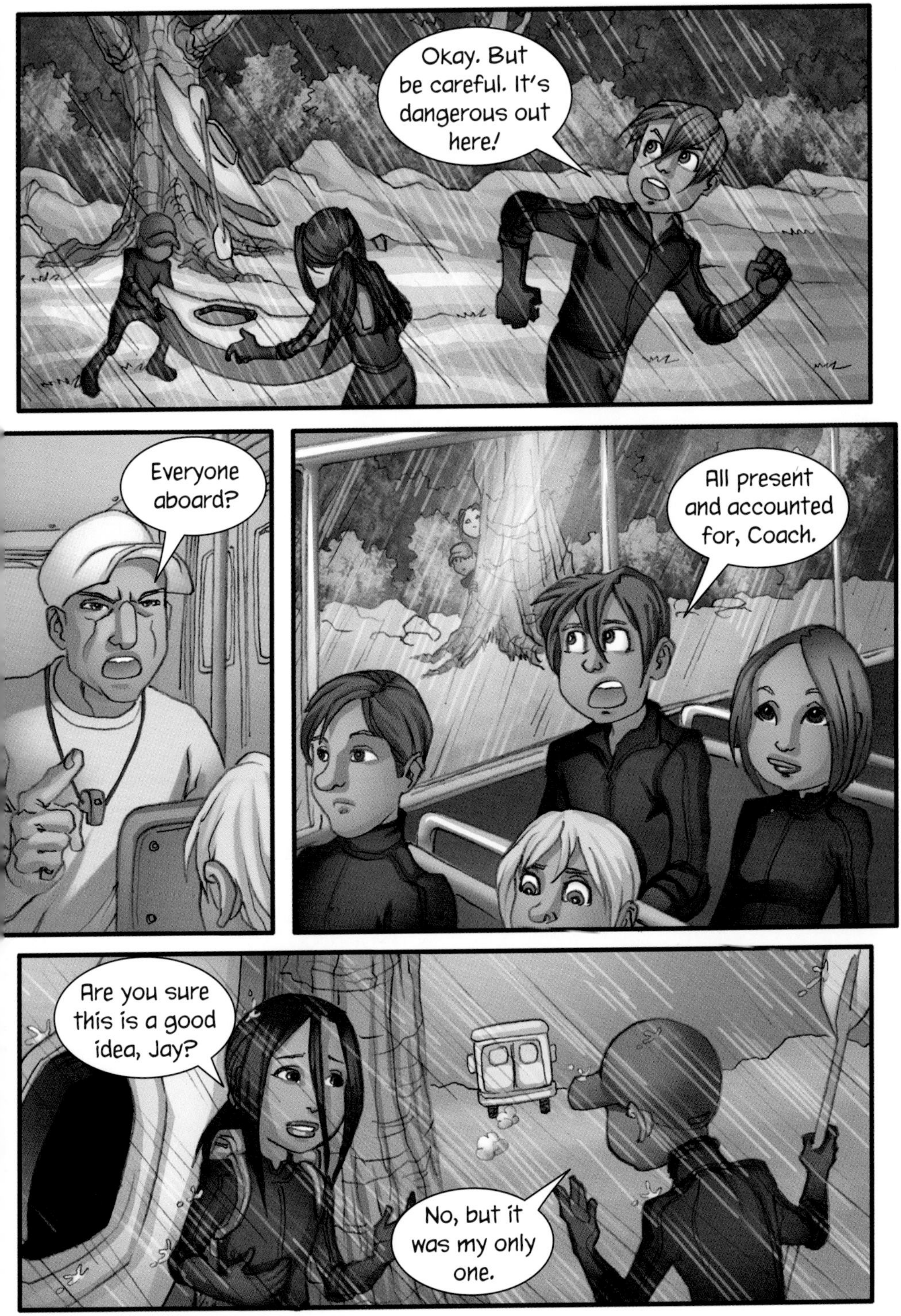
Okay. But be careful. It's dangerous out here!
Everyone aboard?
All present and accounted for, Coach.
Are you sure this is a good idea, Jay?
No, but it was my only one.

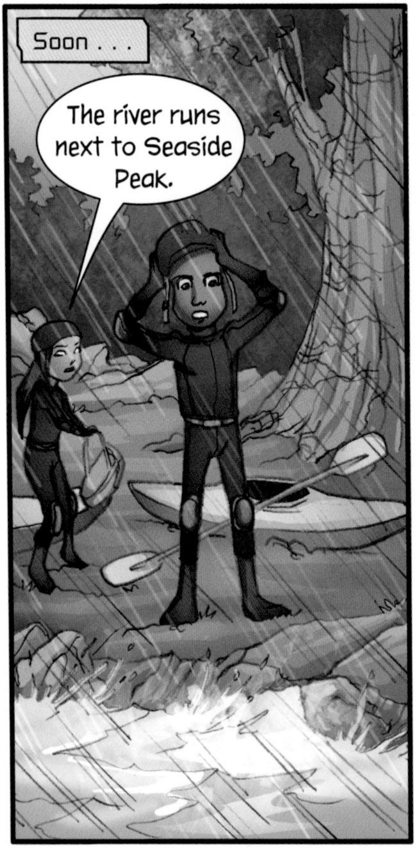
Soon . . .
The river runs next to Seaside Peak.

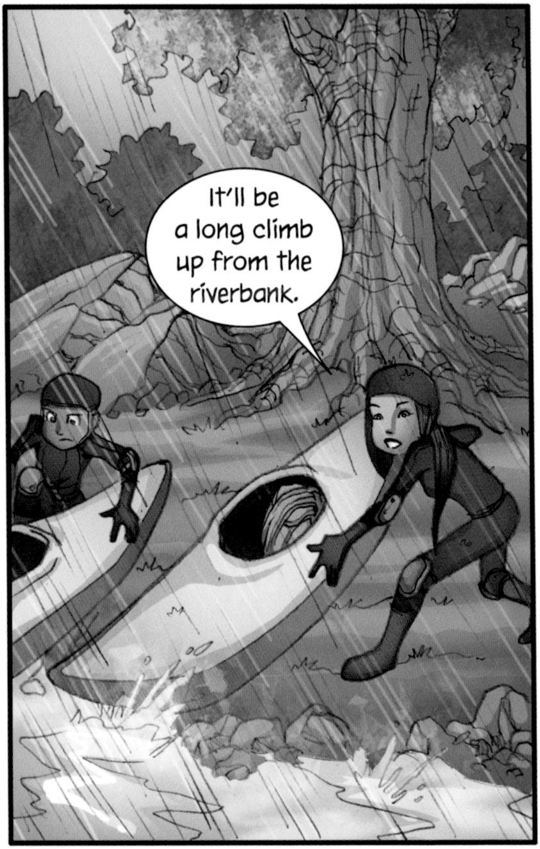
It'll be a long climb up from the riverbank.

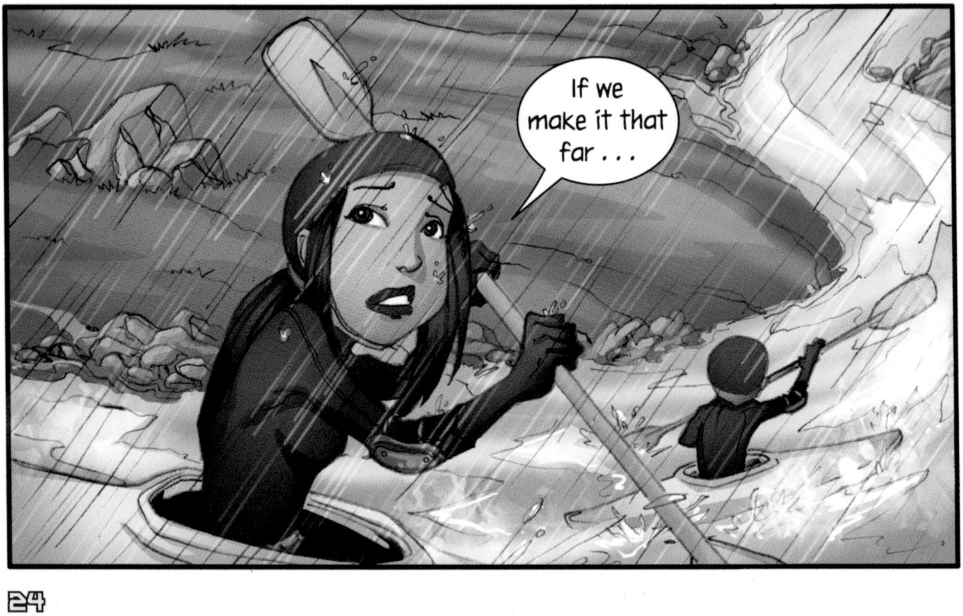
If we make it that far . . .

FILE NO. 1437578

SECTION

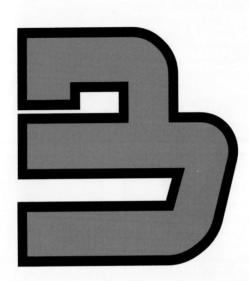

ACCESS GRANTED 〉〉〉

RECON ACADEMY
SECRET SECURITY FORCE

128718
293829
9283
98289
89
1
109201
192091
1992

1827178   198291821   918298

1827178   198291821   918298

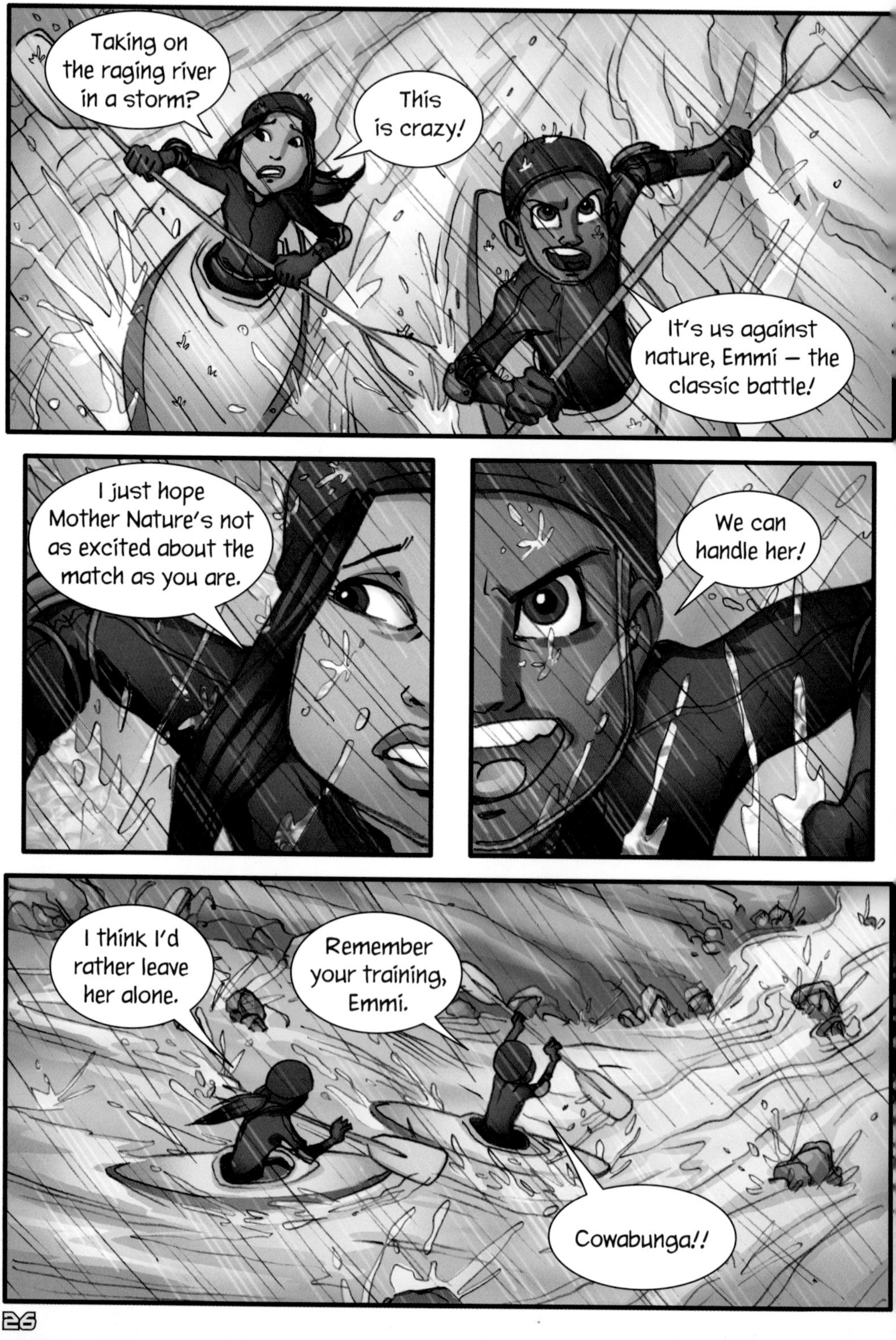
Taking on the raging river in a storm?
This is crazy!
It's us against nature, Emmi — the classic battle!
I just hope Mother Nature's not as excited about the match as you are.
We can handle her!
I think I'd rather leave her alone.
Remember your training, Emmi.
Cowabunga!!

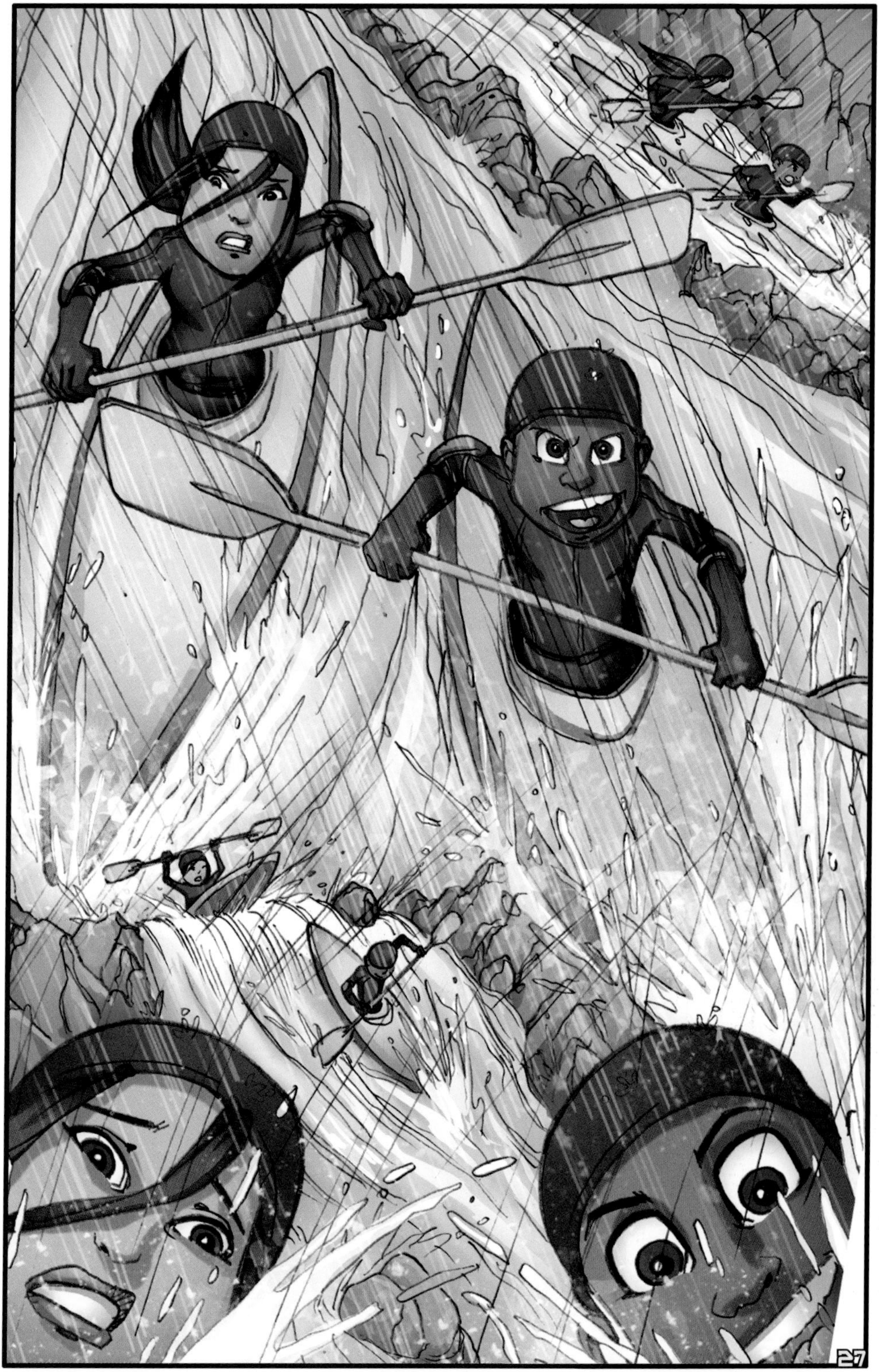

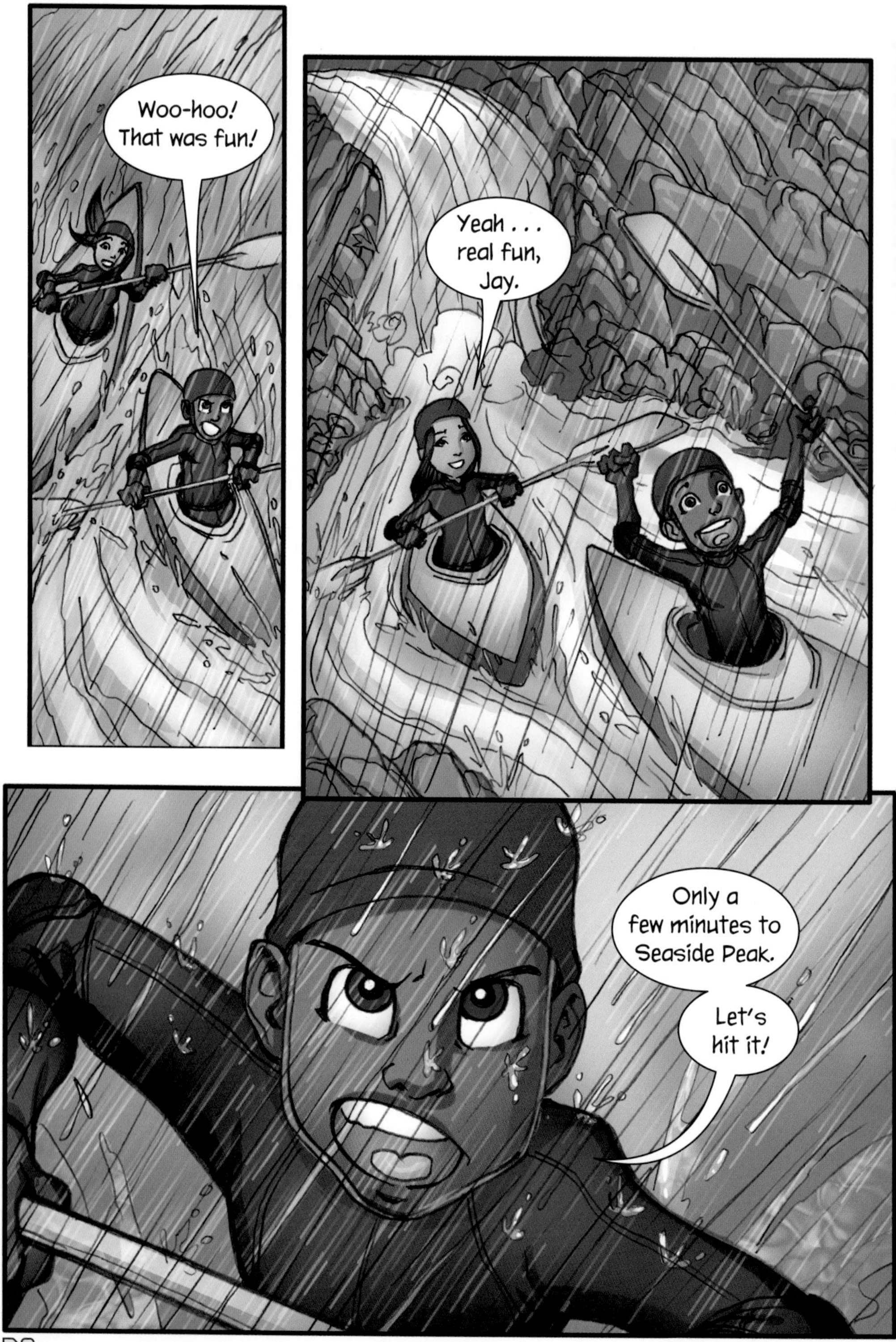
Woo-hoo!
That was fun!
Yeah . . .
real fun,
Jay.
Only a
few minutes to
Seaside Peak.
Let's
hit it!

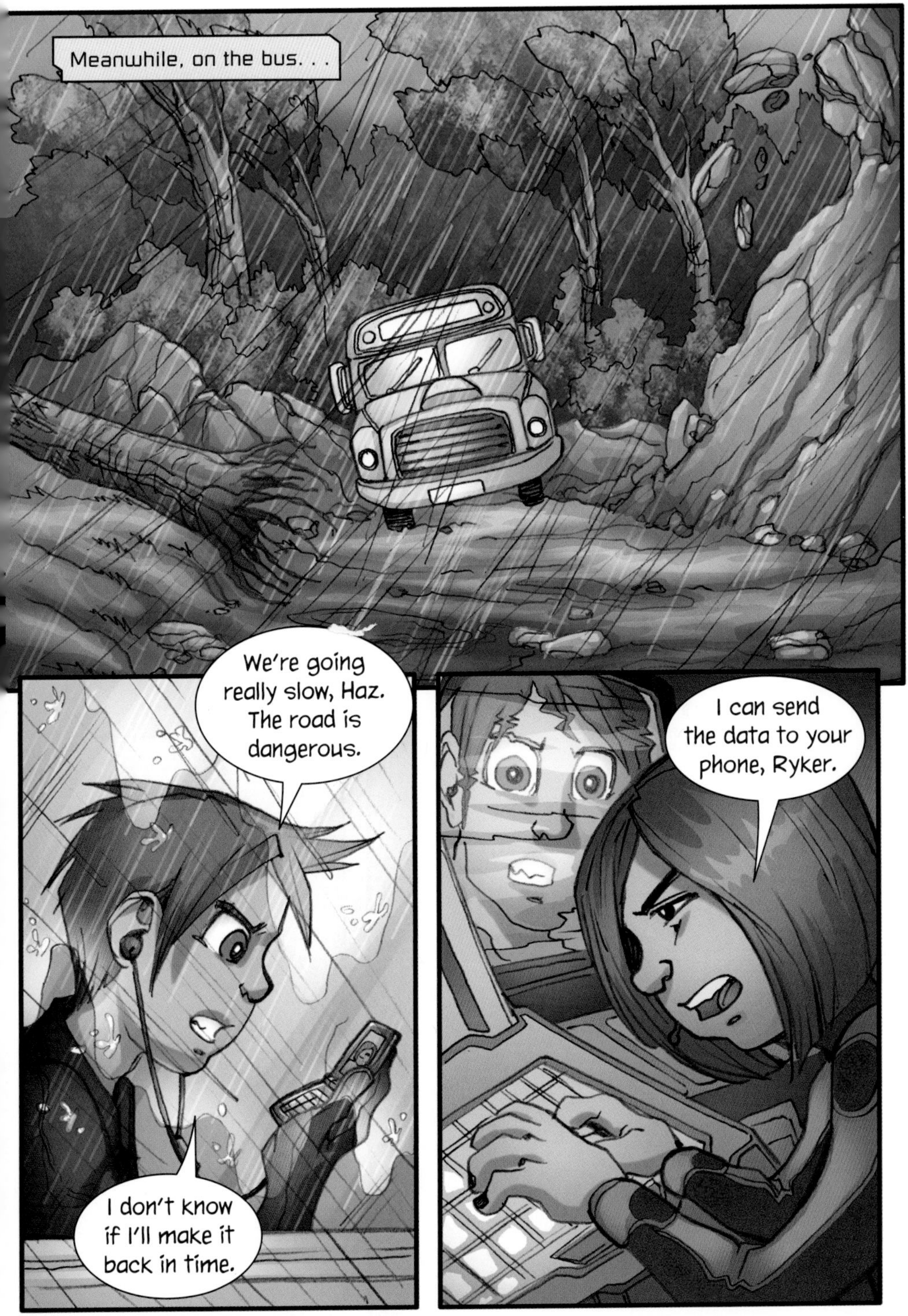
Meanwhile, on the bus. . .
We're going really slow, Haz. The road is dangerous.
I don't know if I'll make it back in time.
I can send the data to your phone, Ryker.

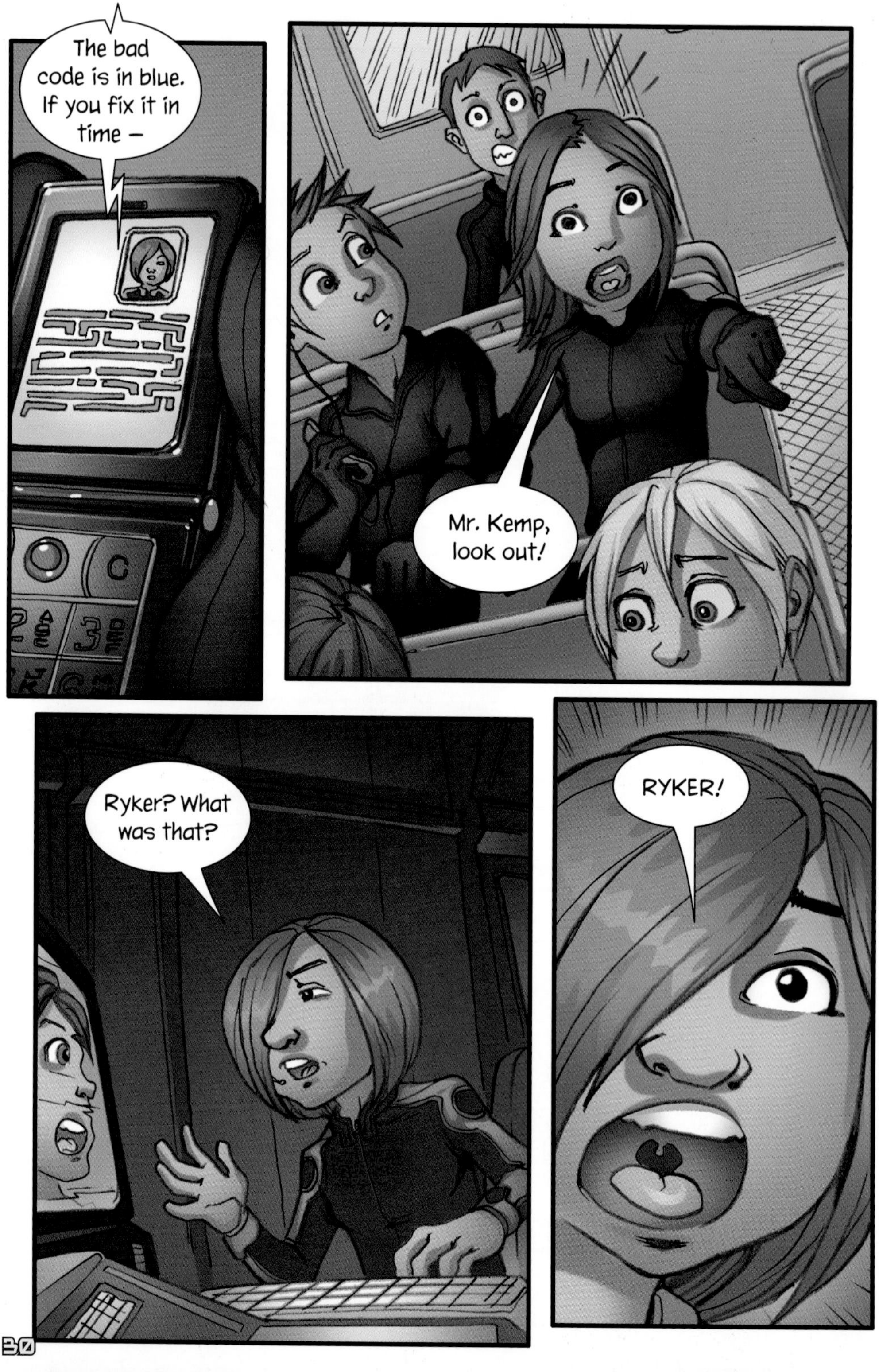

The bad code is in blue. If you fix it in time –
Mr. Kemp, look out!
Ryker? What was that?
RYKER!

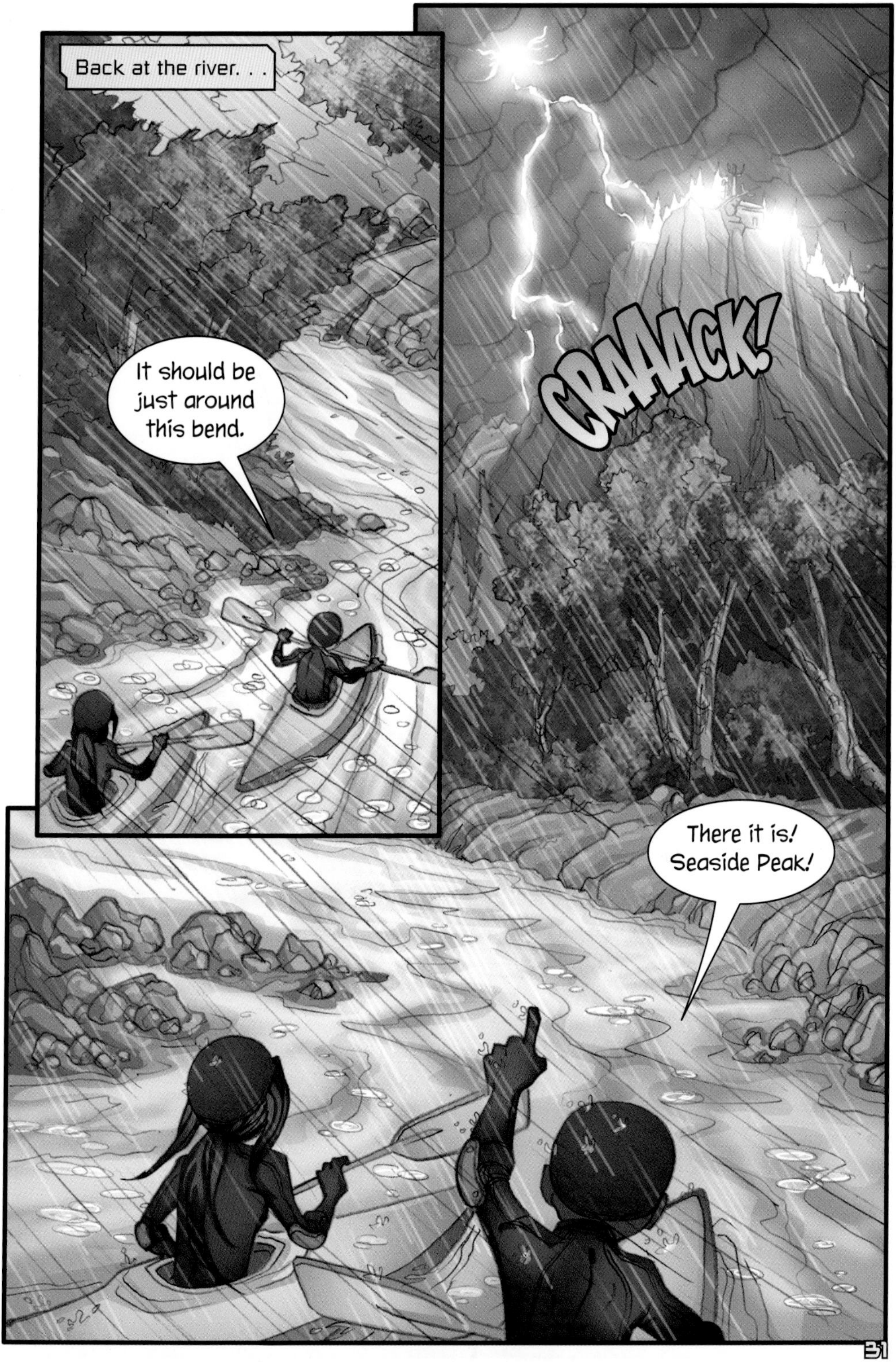
Back at the river. . .
It should be just around this bend.
CRAAACK!
There it is! Seaside Peak!

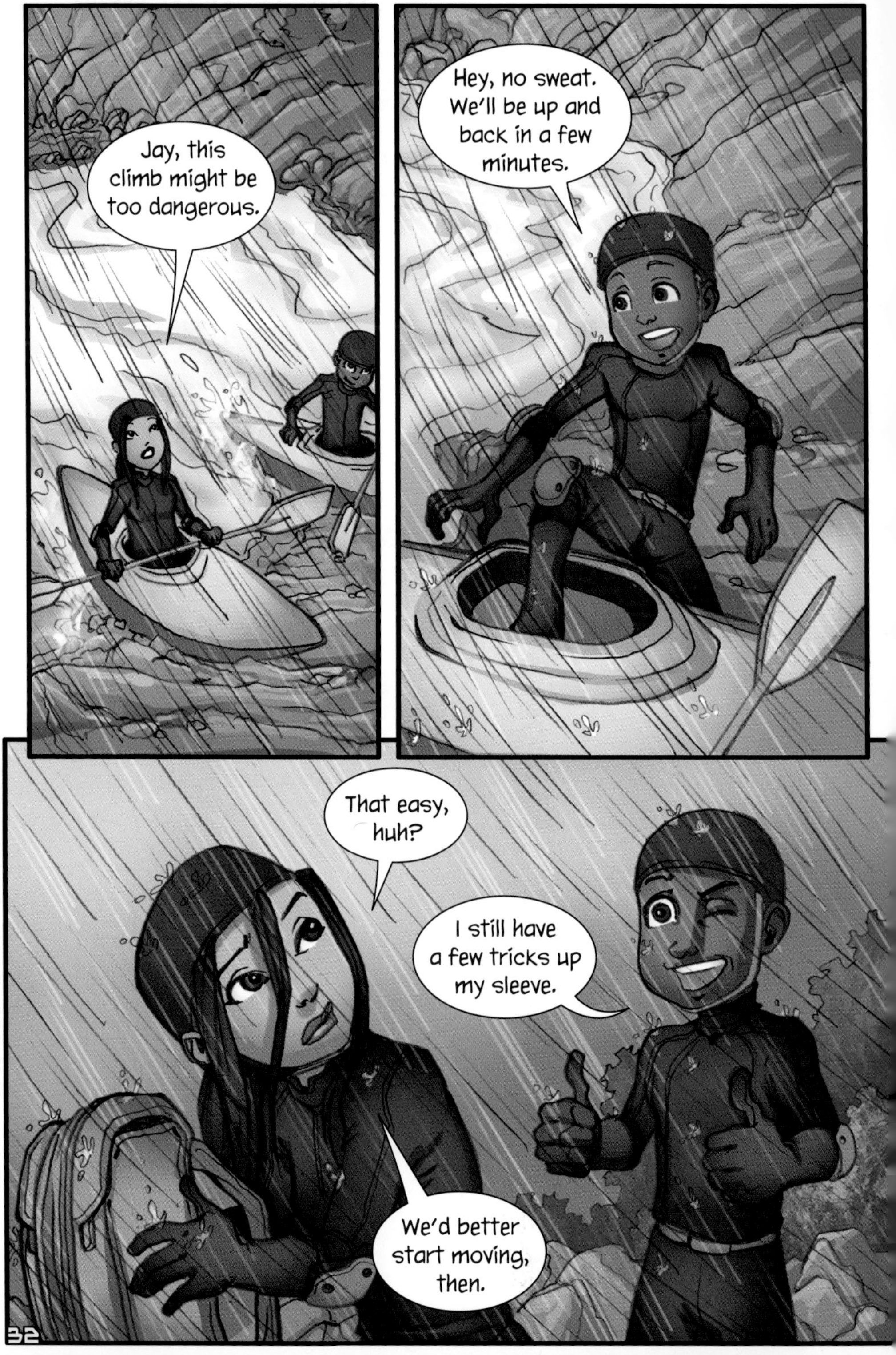

Jay, this climb might be too dangerous.
Hey, no sweat. We'll be up and back in a few minutes.
That easy, huh?
I still have a few tricks up my sleeve.
We'd better start moving, then.

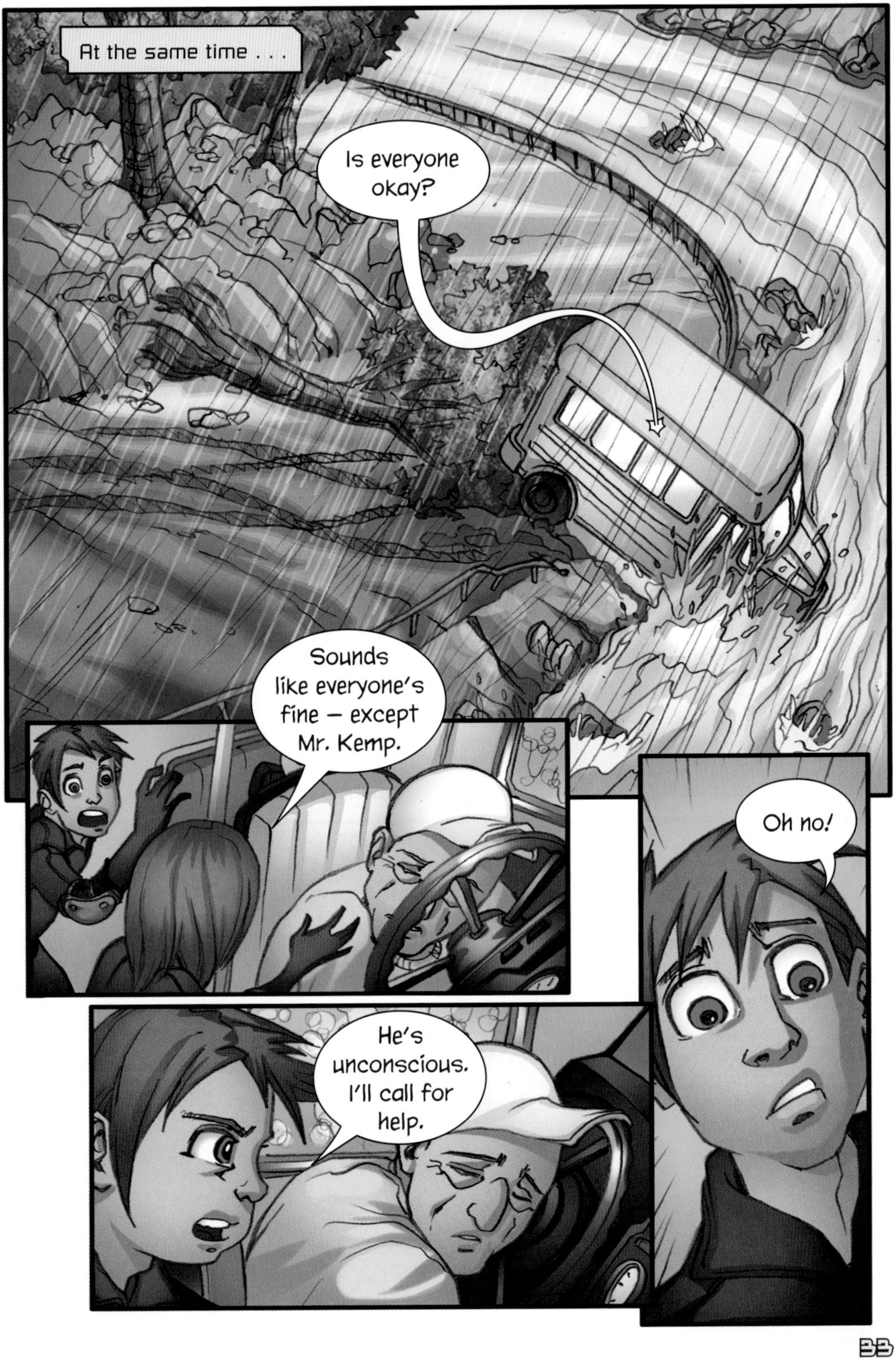
At the same time . . .
Is everyone okay?
Sounds like everyone's fine – except Mr. Kemp.
Oh no!
He's unconscious. I'll call for help.

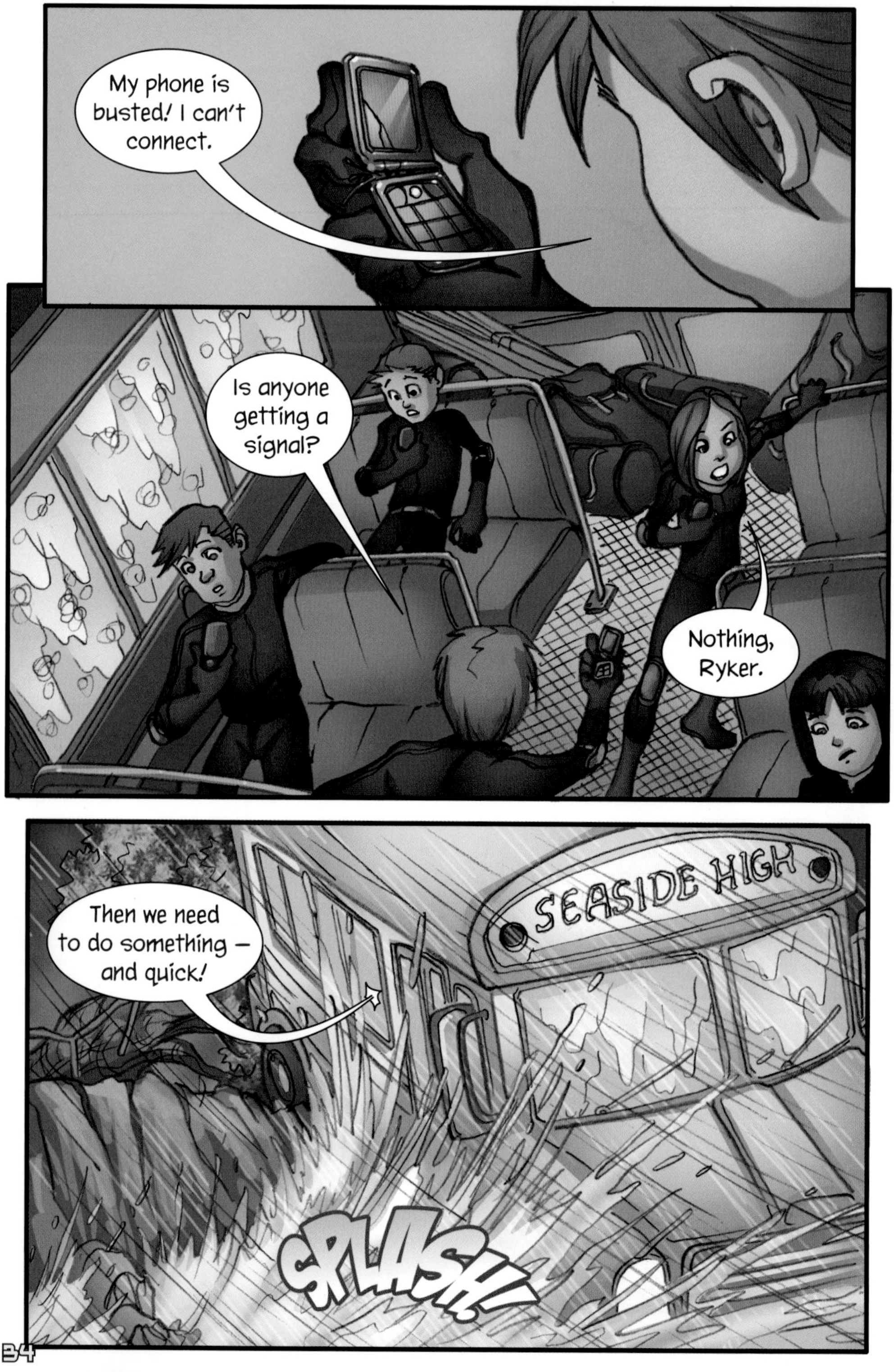
My phone is busted! I can't connect.
Is anyone getting a signal?
Nothing, Ryker.
SEASIDE HIGH
Then we need to do something — and quick!
SPLASH!

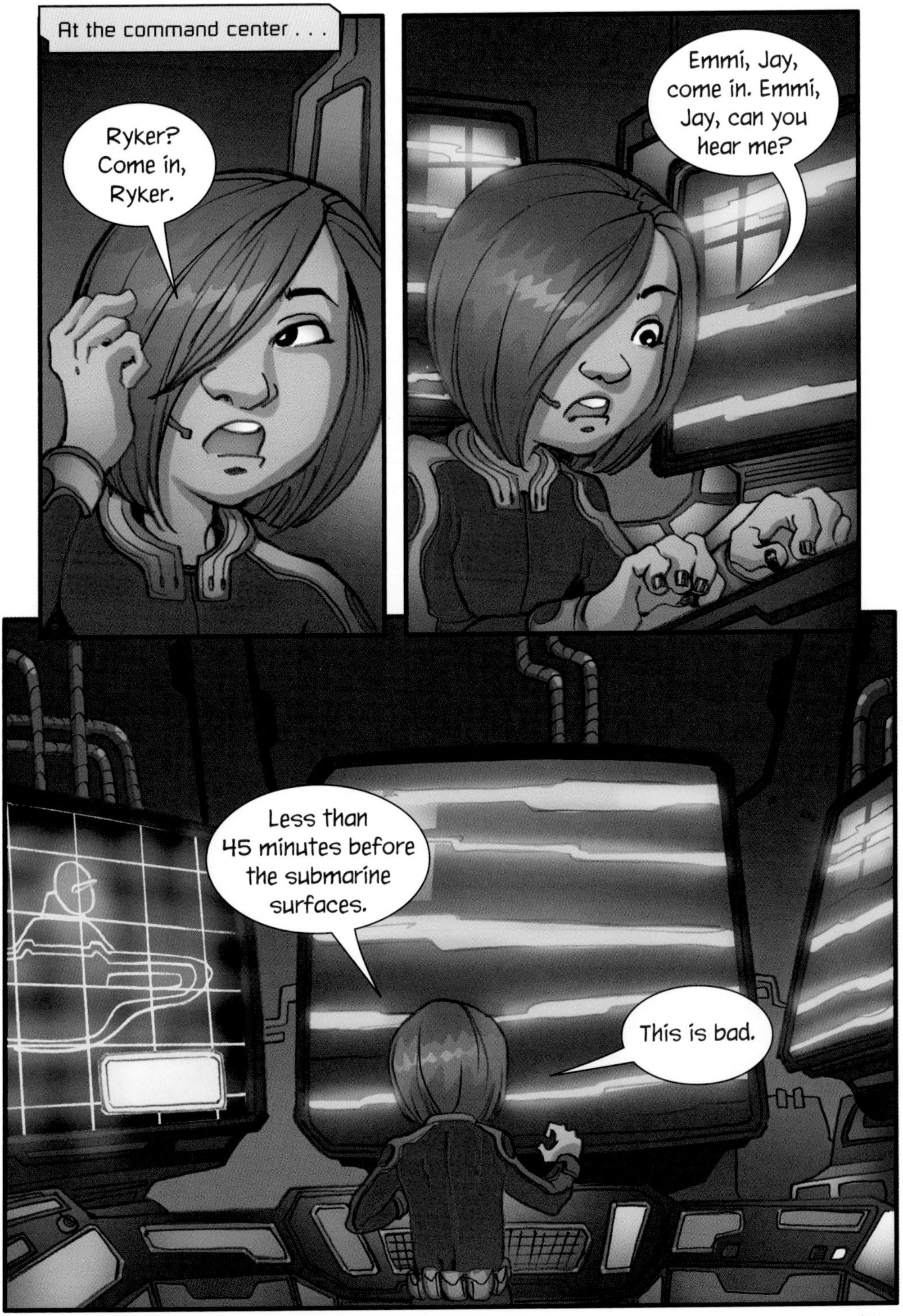
At the command center . . .
Ryker? Come in, Ryker.
Emmi, Jay, come in. Emmi, Jay, can you hear me?
Less than 45 minutes before the submarine surfaces.
This is bad.

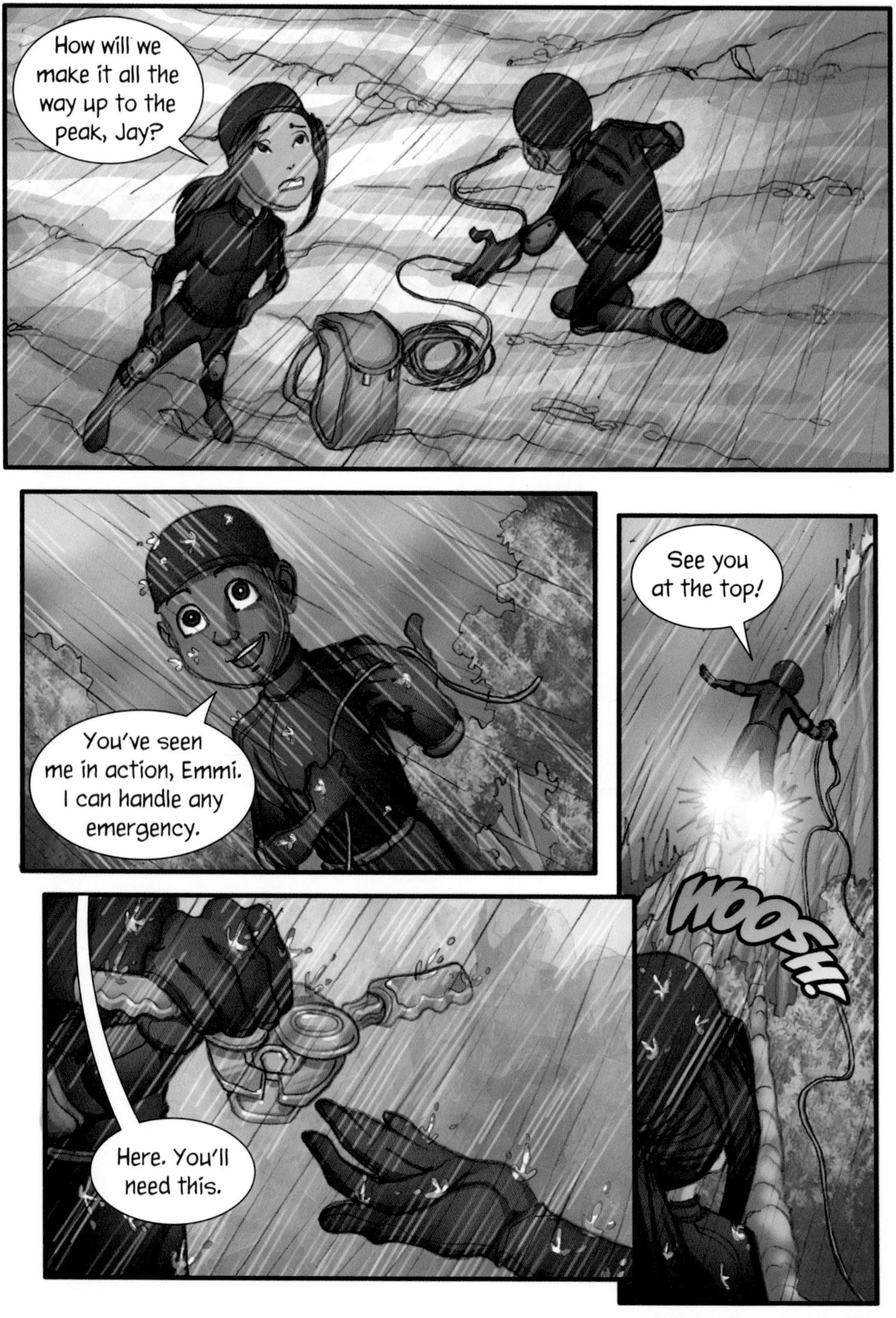
How will we make it all the way up to the peak, Jay?
You've seen me in action, Emmi. I can handle any emergency.
See you at the top!
Here. You'll need this.
WOOSH!

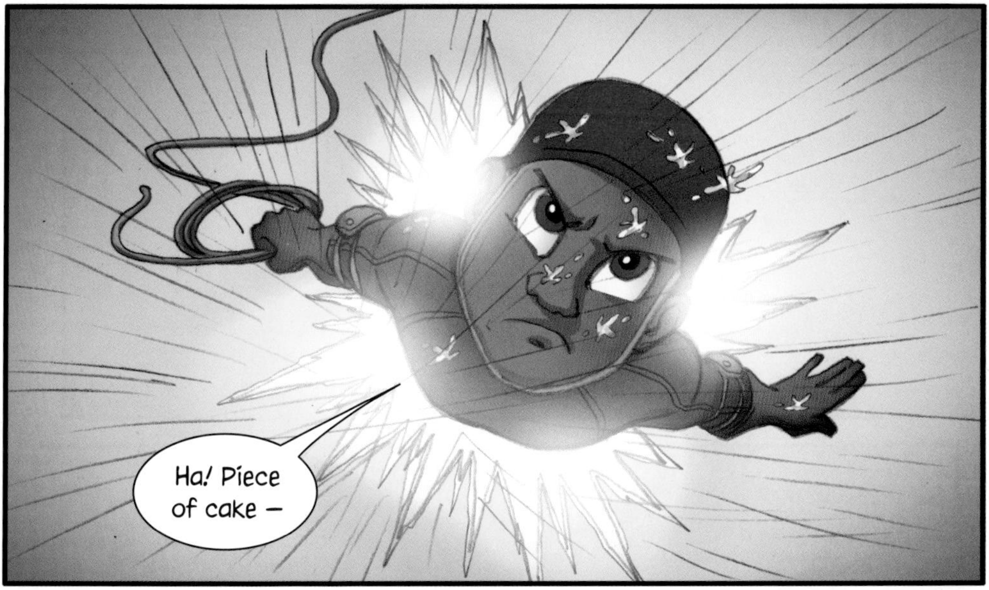
Ha! Piece of cake —

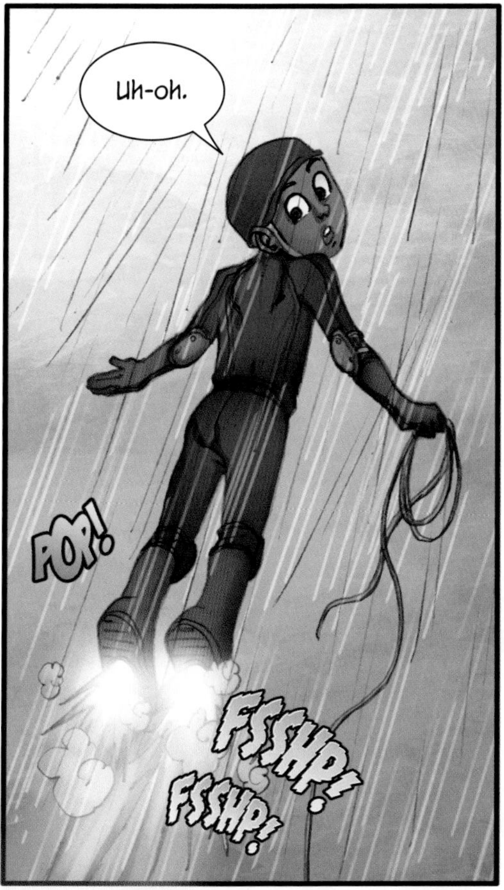
Uh-oh.
POP!
FSSHP!
FSSHP!

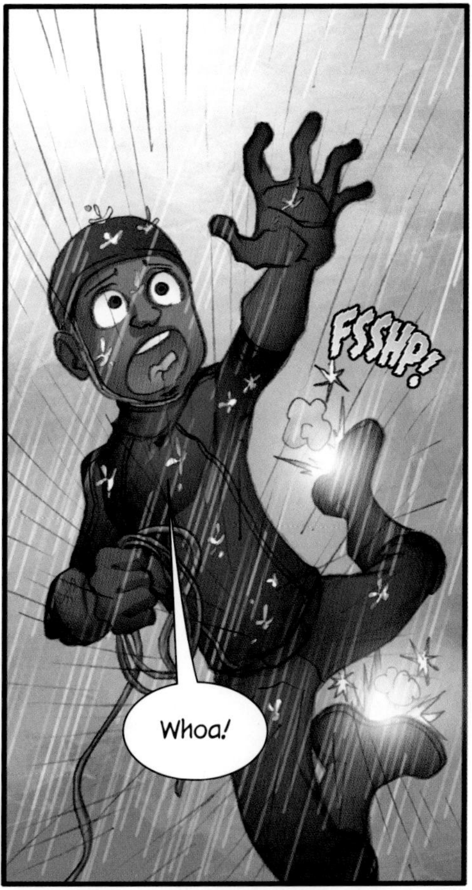
FSSHP!
Whoa!

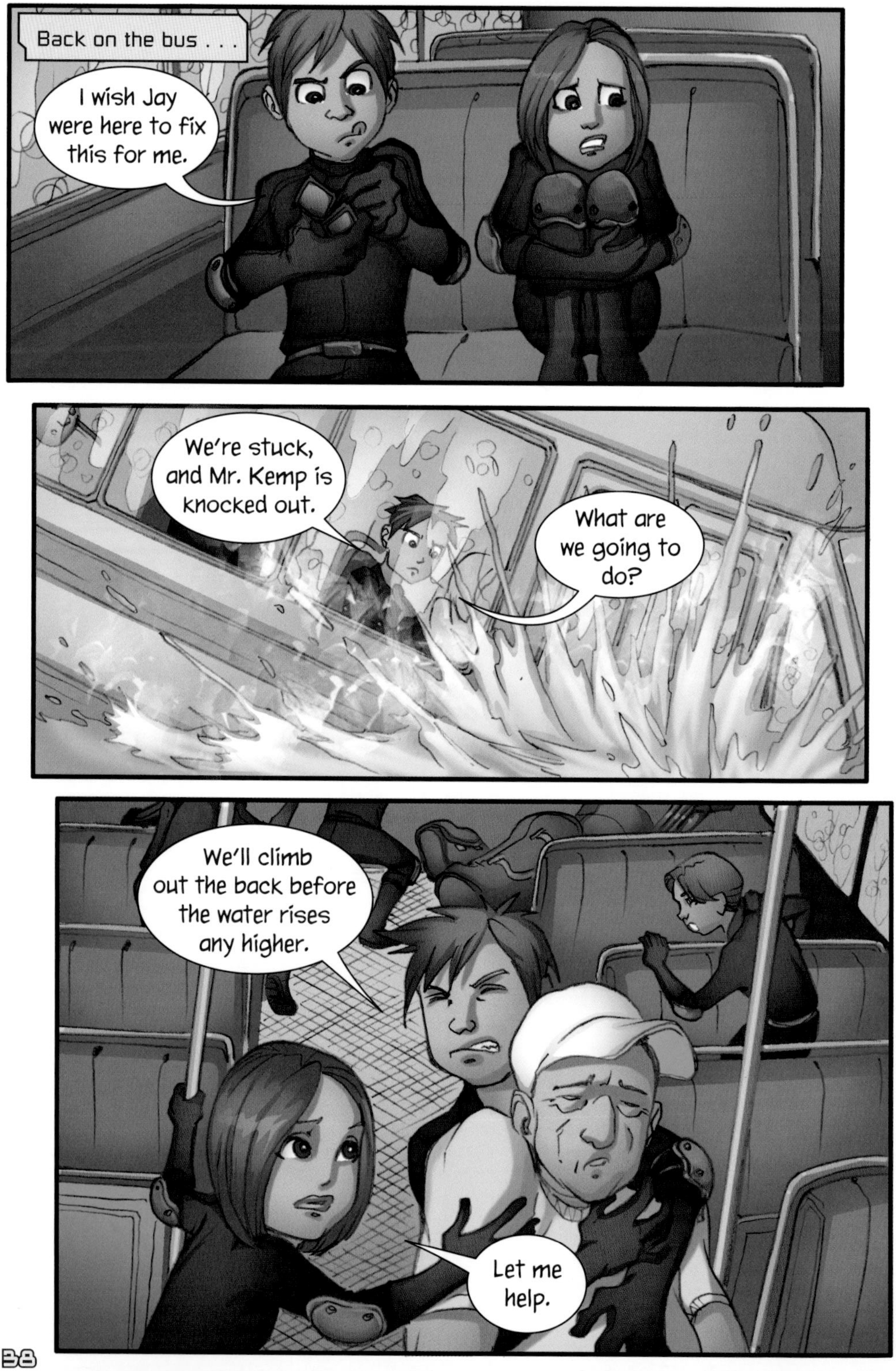

Back on the bus . . .
I wish Jay were here to fix this for me.
We're stuck, and Mr. Kemp is knocked out.
What are we going to do?
We'll climb out the back before the water rises any higher.
Let me help.

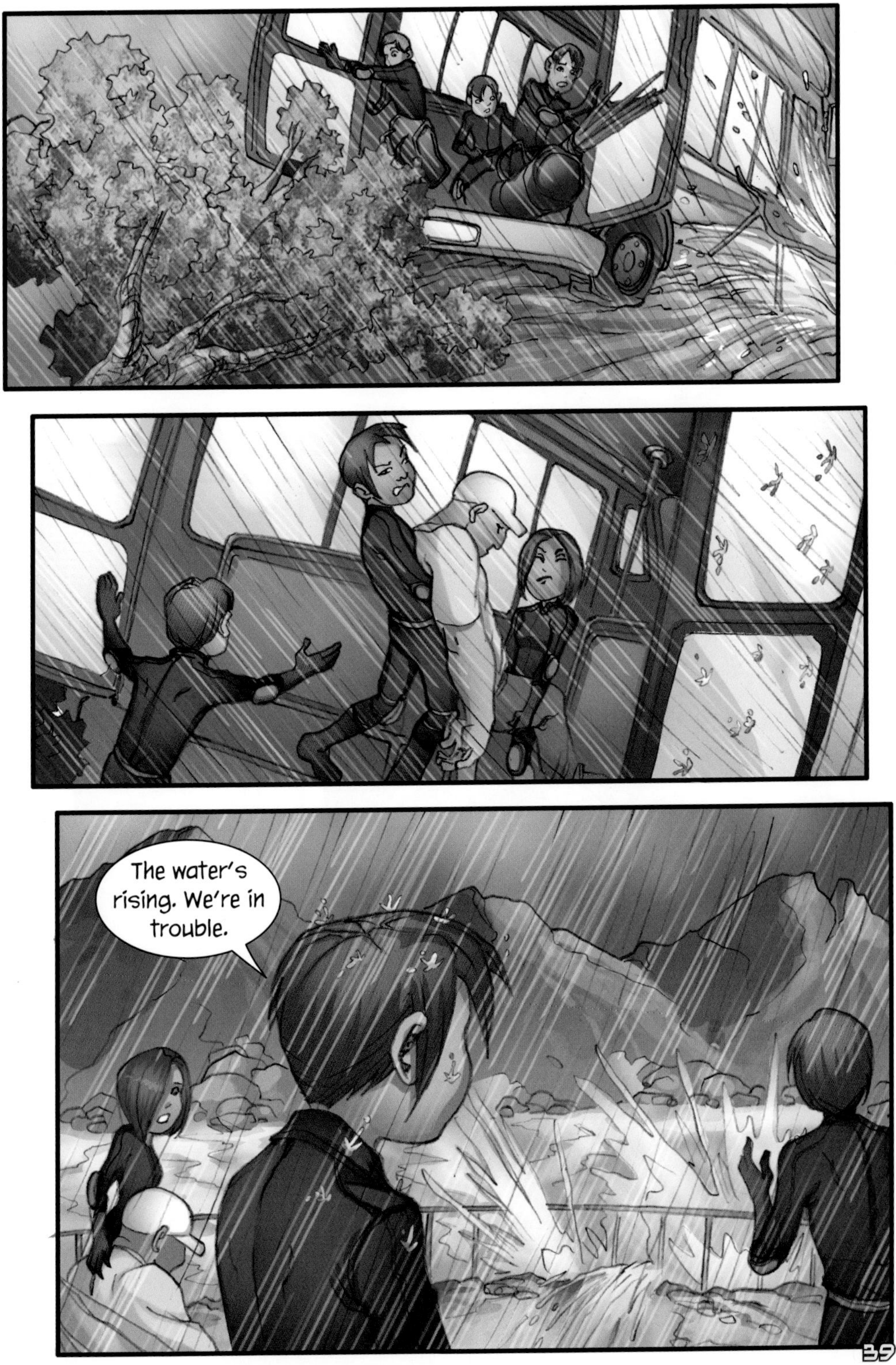
The water's rising. We're in trouble.

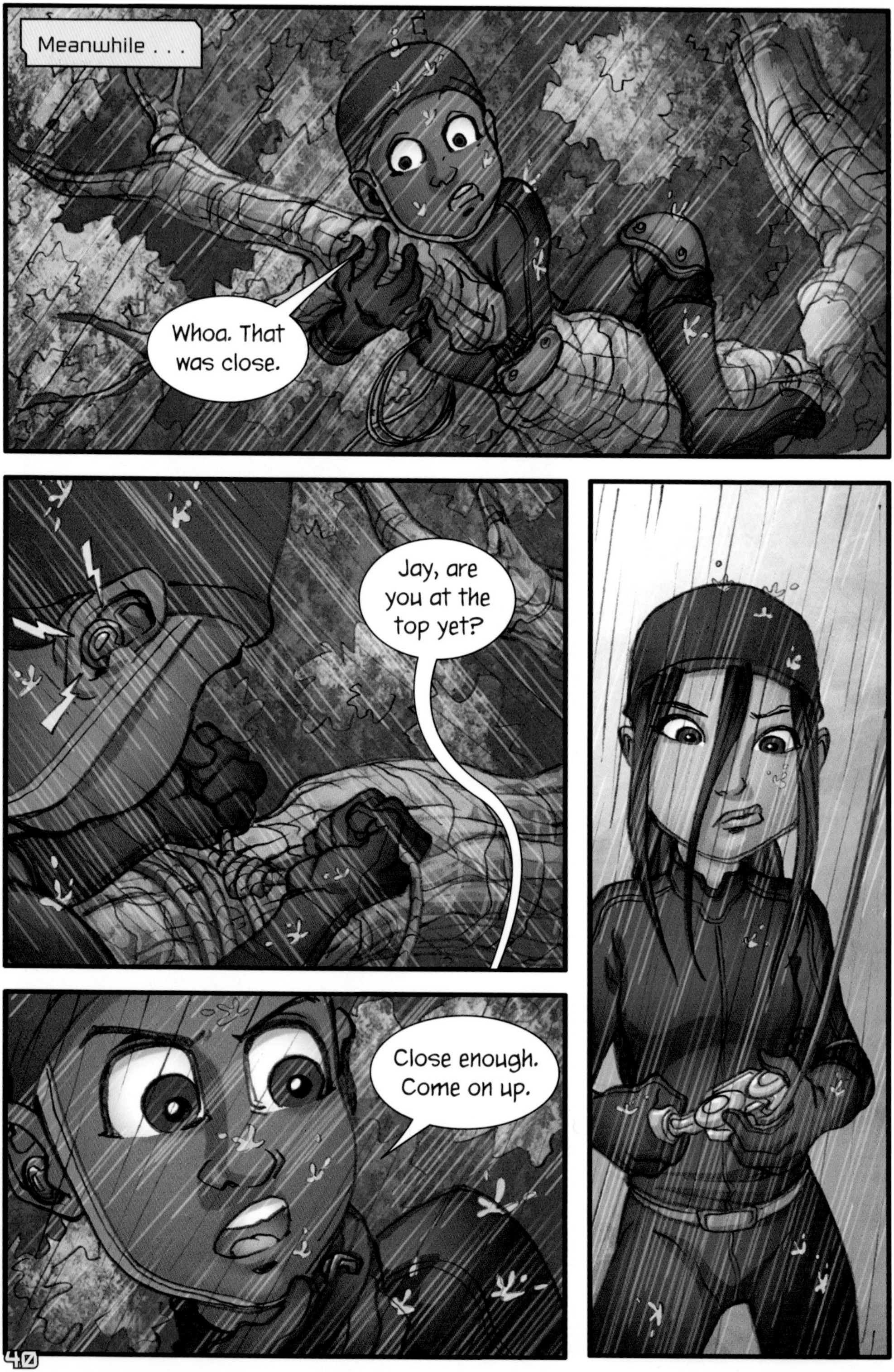
Meanwhile . . .
Whoa. That was close.
Jay, are you at the top yet?
Close enough. Come on up.

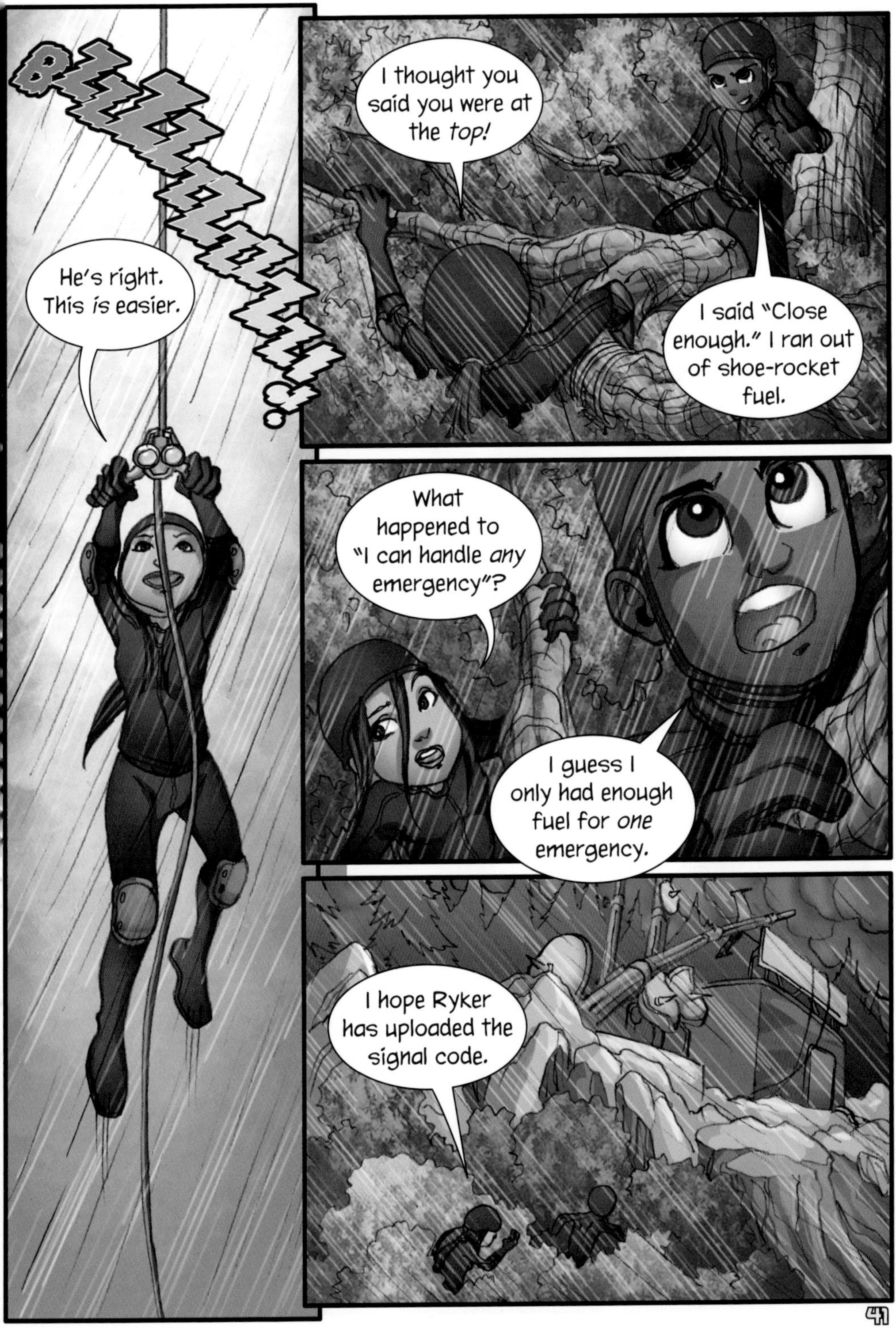
BZZZZZZZZZZZ!
He's right. This *is* easier.
I thought you said you were at the *top!*
I said "Close enough." I ran out of shoe-rocket fuel.
What happened to "I can handle *any* emergency"?
I guess I only had enough fuel for *one* emergency.
I hope Ryker has uploaded the signal code.

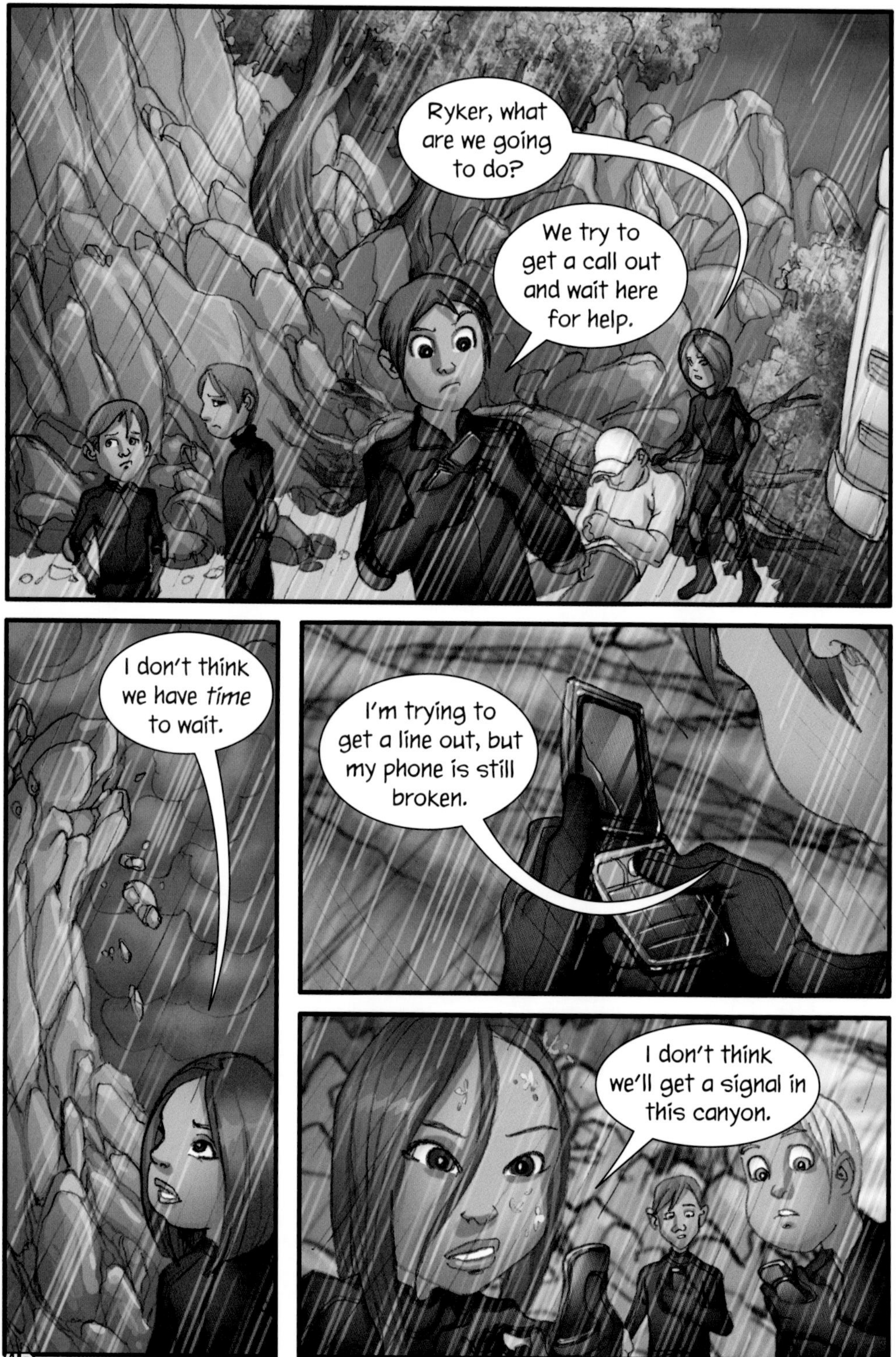
Ryker, what are we going to do?
We try to get a call out and wait here for help.
I don't think we have *time* to wait.
I'm trying to get a line out, but my phone is still broken.
I don't think we'll get a signal in this canyon.

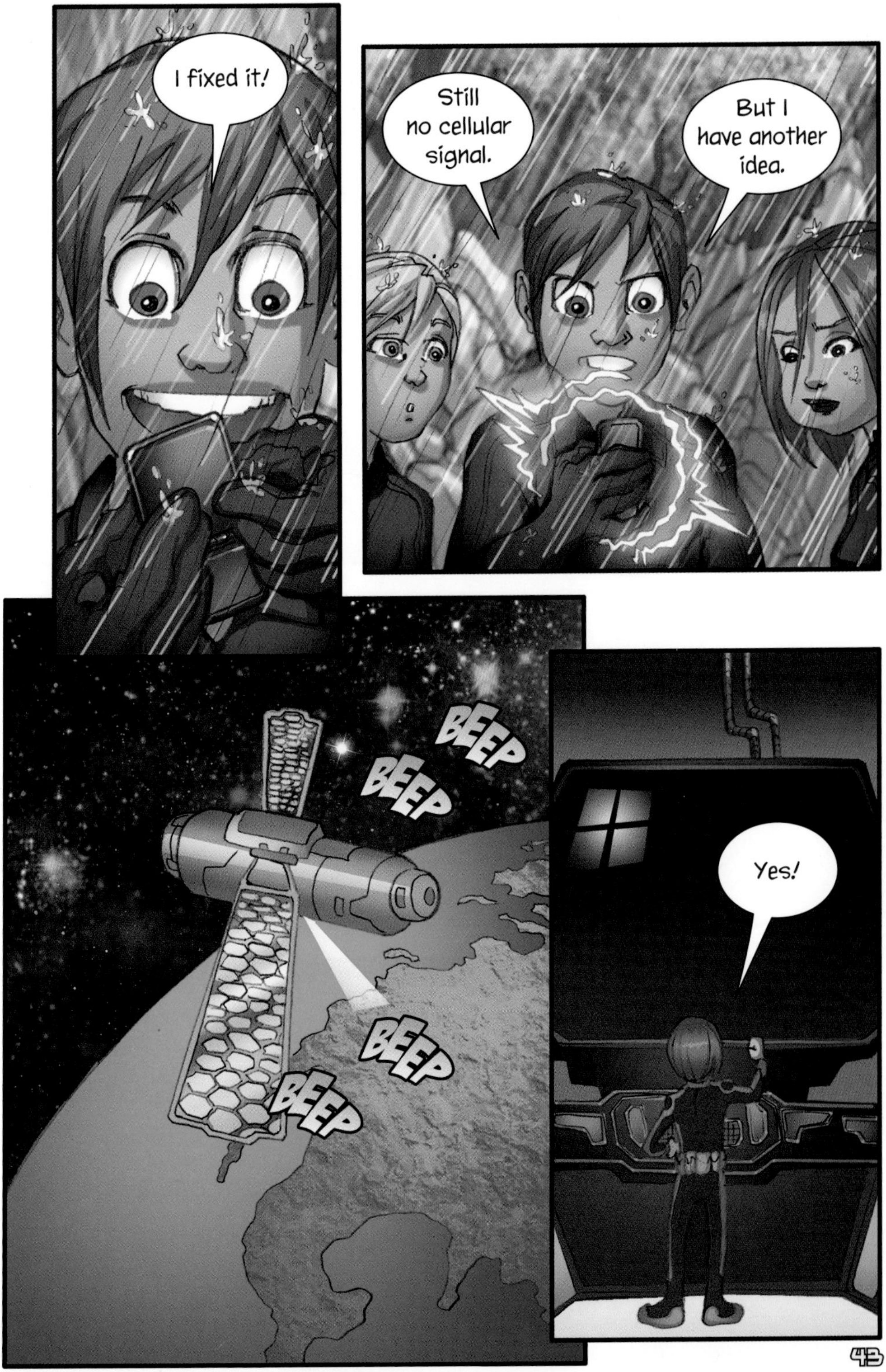
I fixed it!
Still no cellular signal.
But I have another idea.
BEEP
BEEP
BEEP
BEEP
Yes!

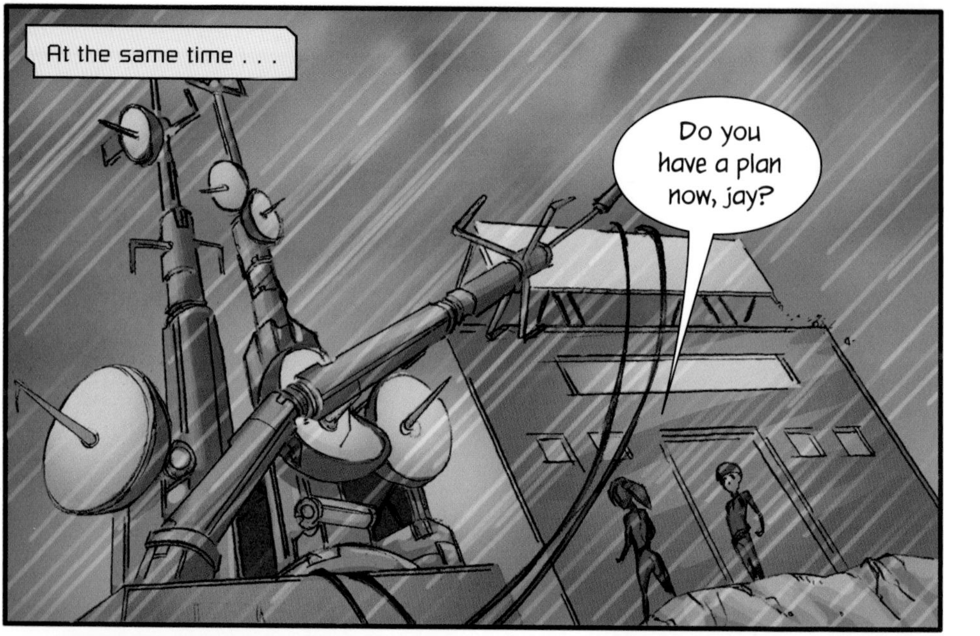
At the same time . . .
Do you have a plan now, jay?

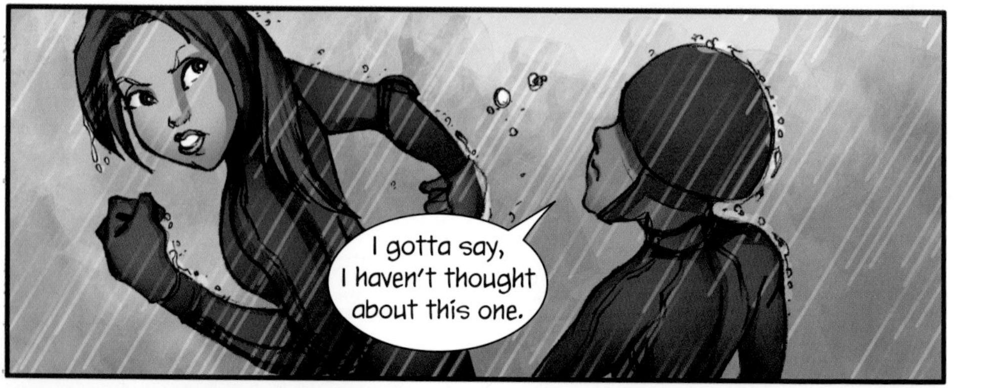
I gotta say, I haven't thought about this one.

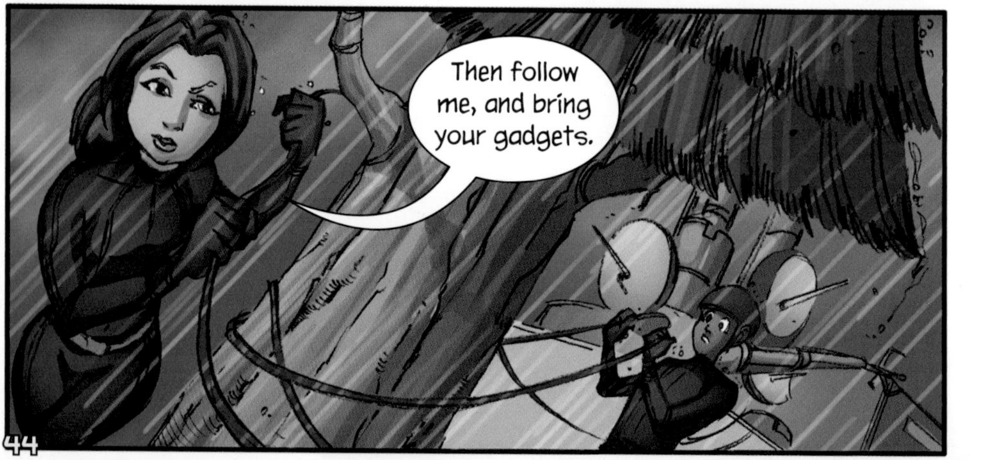
Then follow me, and bring your gadgets.

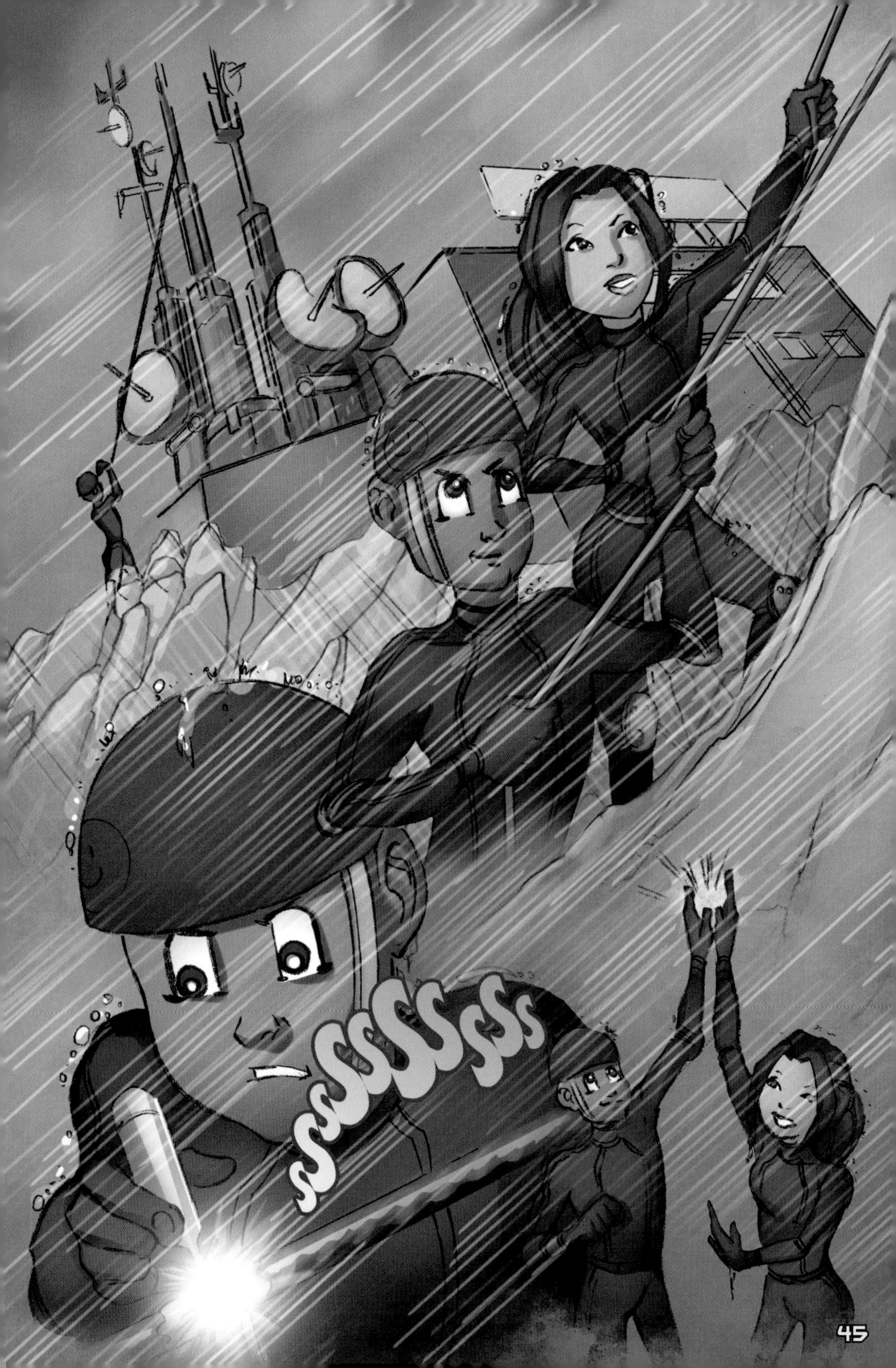
ssSSSss

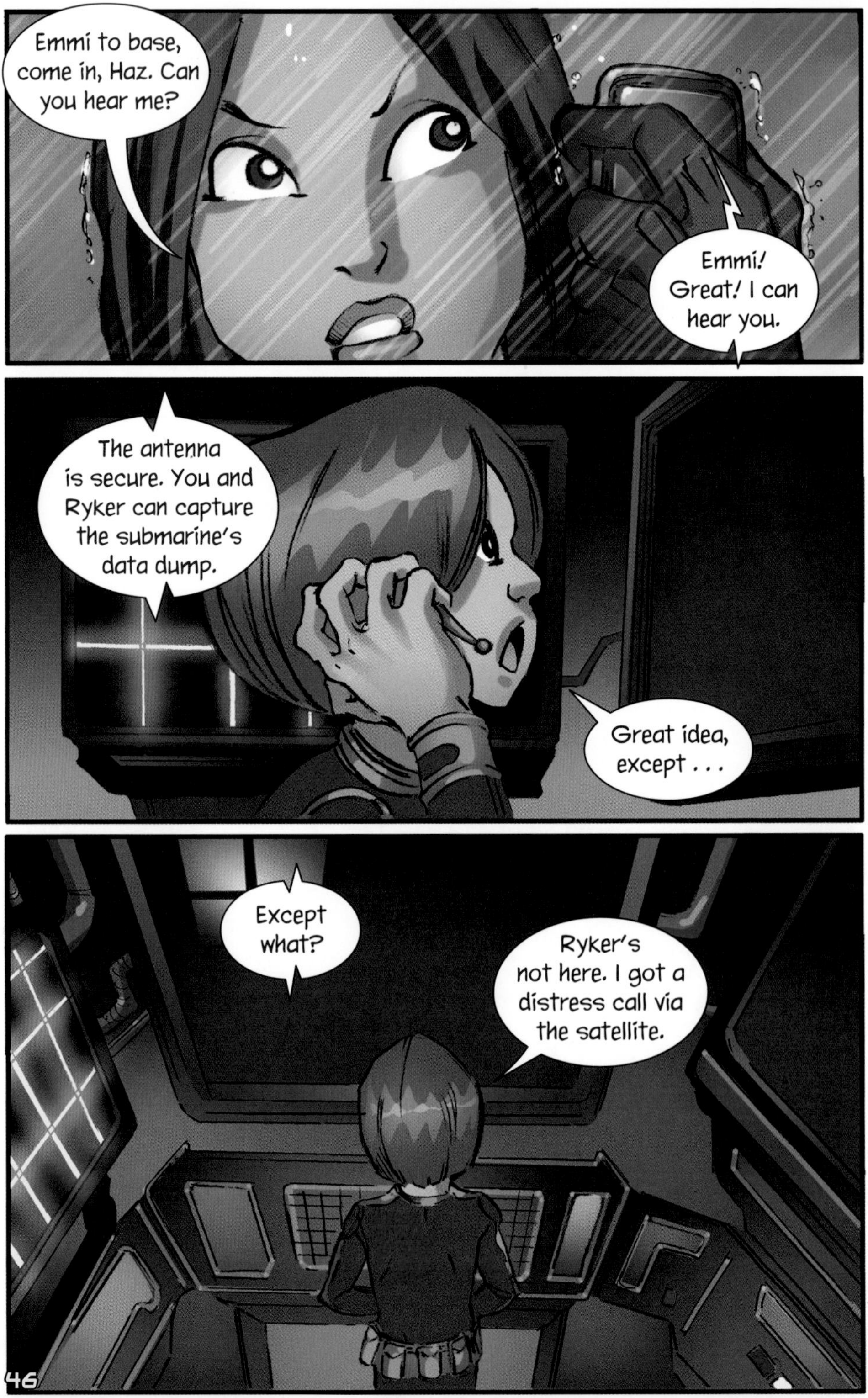
Emmi to base, come in, Haz. Can you hear me?
Emmi! Great! I can hear you.
The antenna is secure. You and Ryker can capture the submarine's data dump.
Great idea, except . . .
Except what?
Ryker's not here. I got a distress call via the satellite.

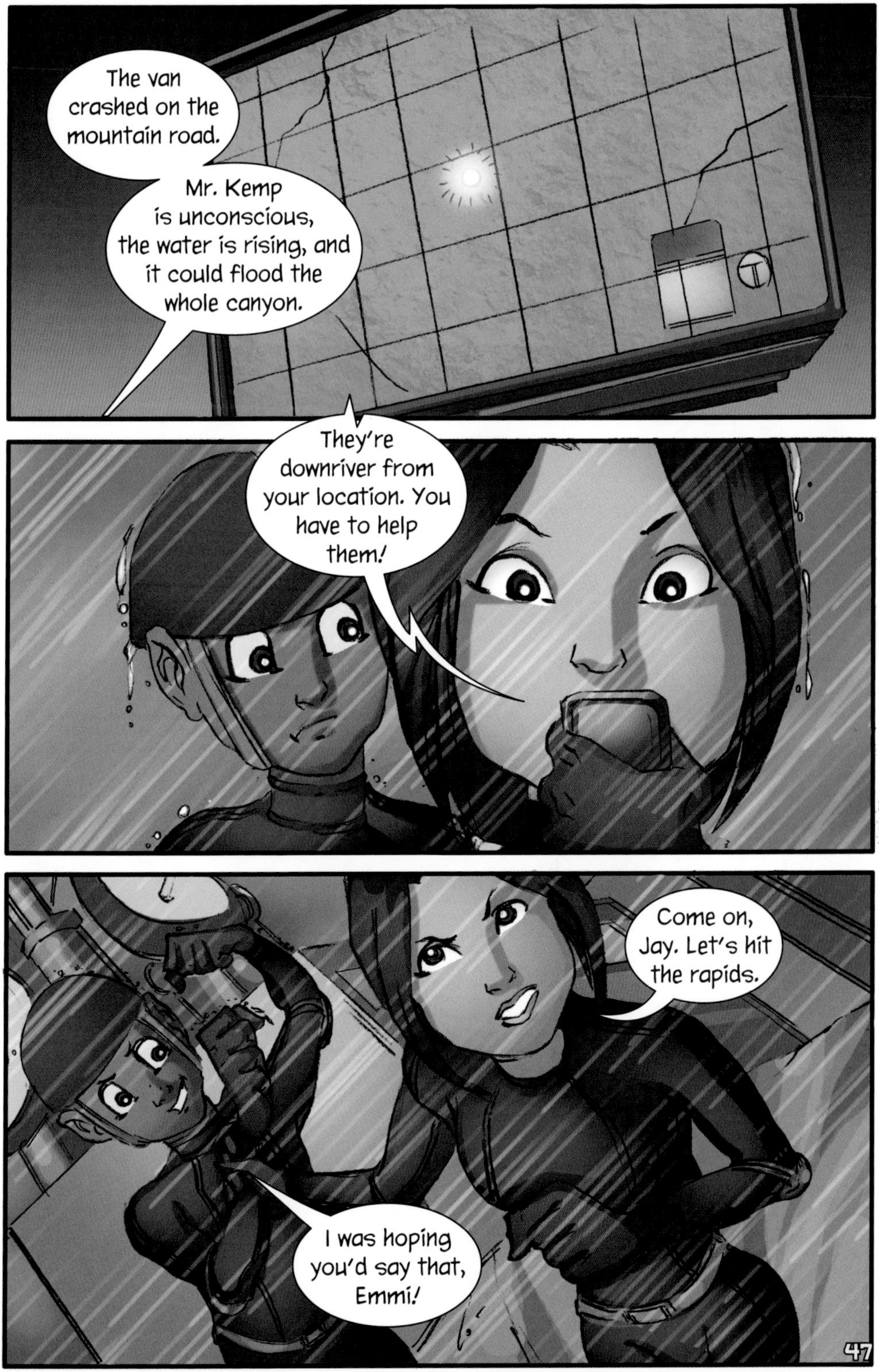
The van crashed on the mountain road.
Mr. Kemp is unconscious, the water is rising, and it could flood the whole canyon.
They're downriver from your location. You have to help them!
Come on, Jay. Let's hit the rapids.
I was hoping you'd say that, Emmi!

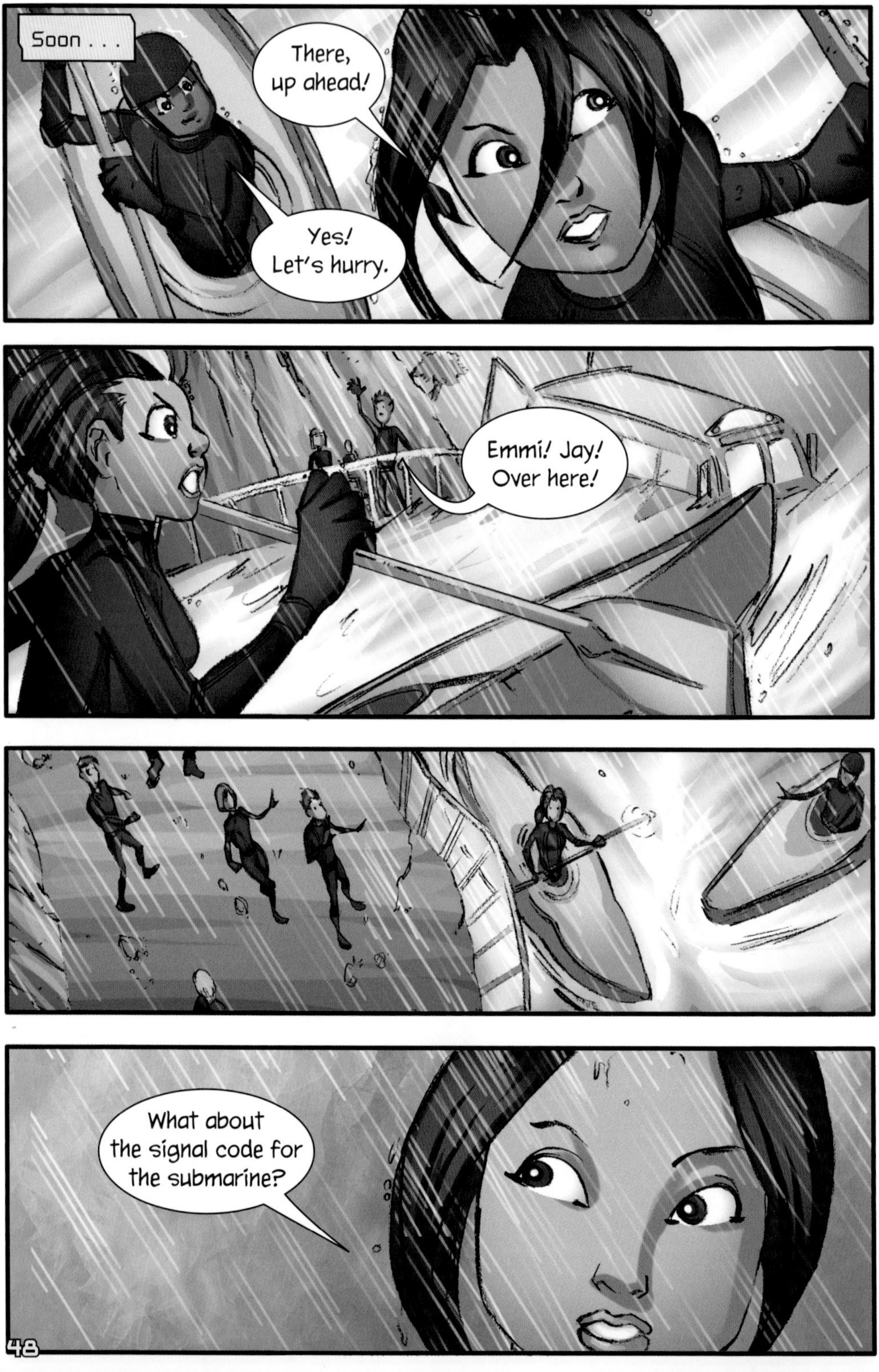
Soon . . .
There, up ahead!
Yes! Let's hurry.
Emmi! Jay! Over here!
What about the signal code for the submarine?

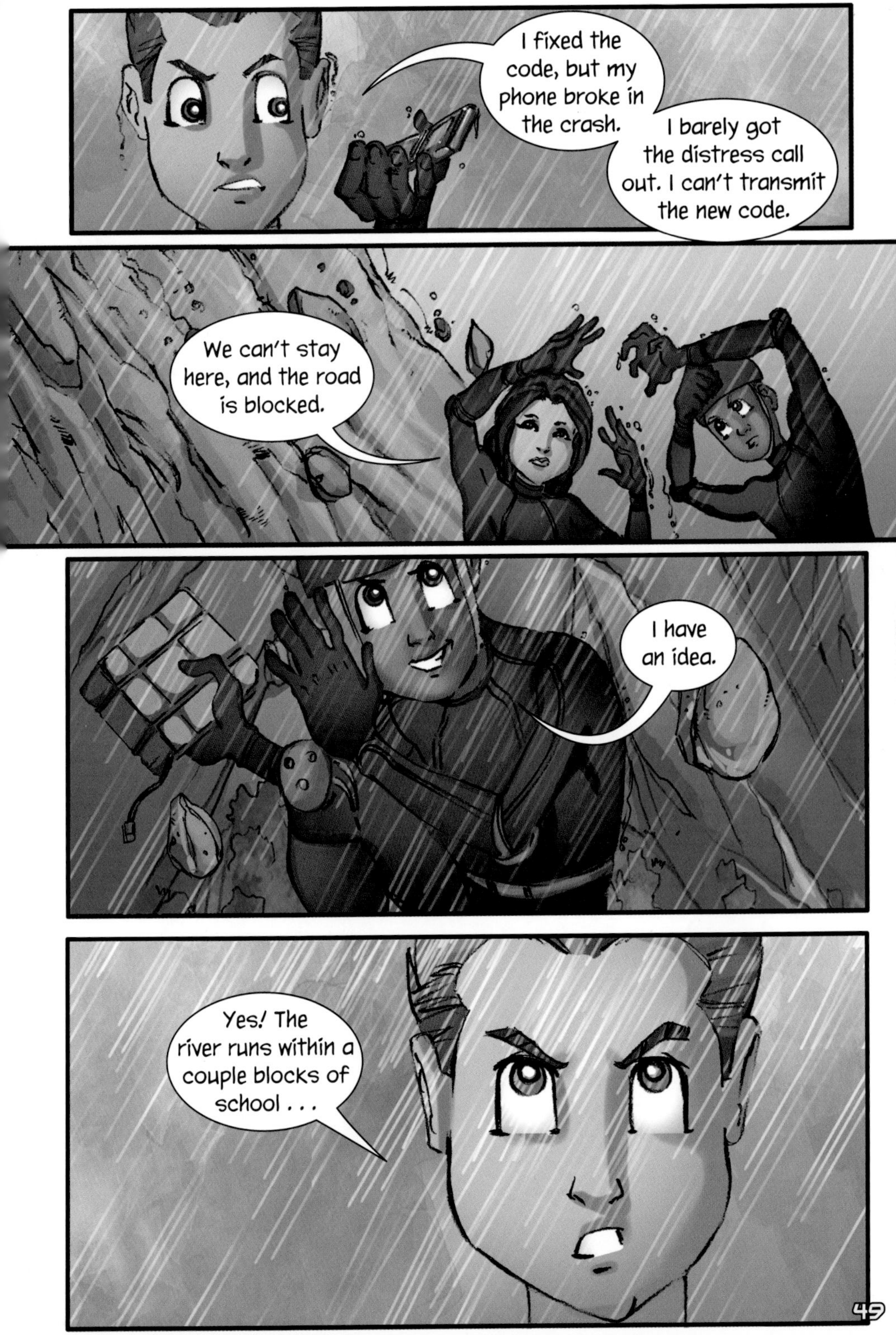
I fixed the code, but my phone broke in the crash.
I barely got the distress call out. I can't transmit the new code.
We can't stay here, and the road is blocked.
I have an idea.
Yes! The river runs within a couple blocks of school . . .

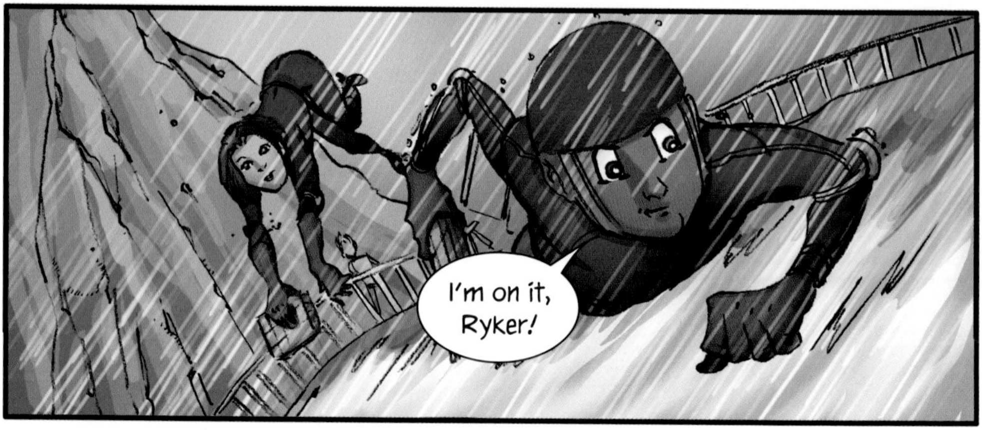
I'm on it,
Ryker!

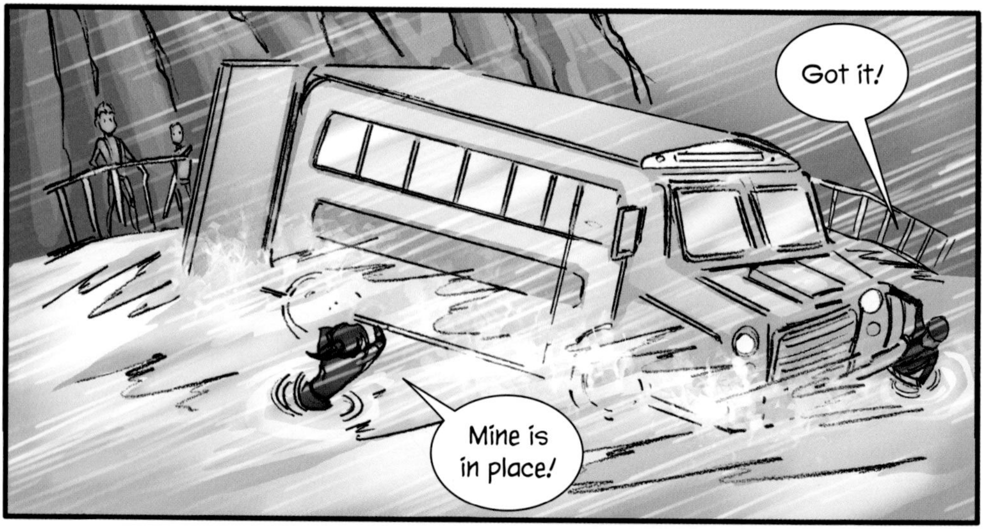
Got it!
Mine is
in place!

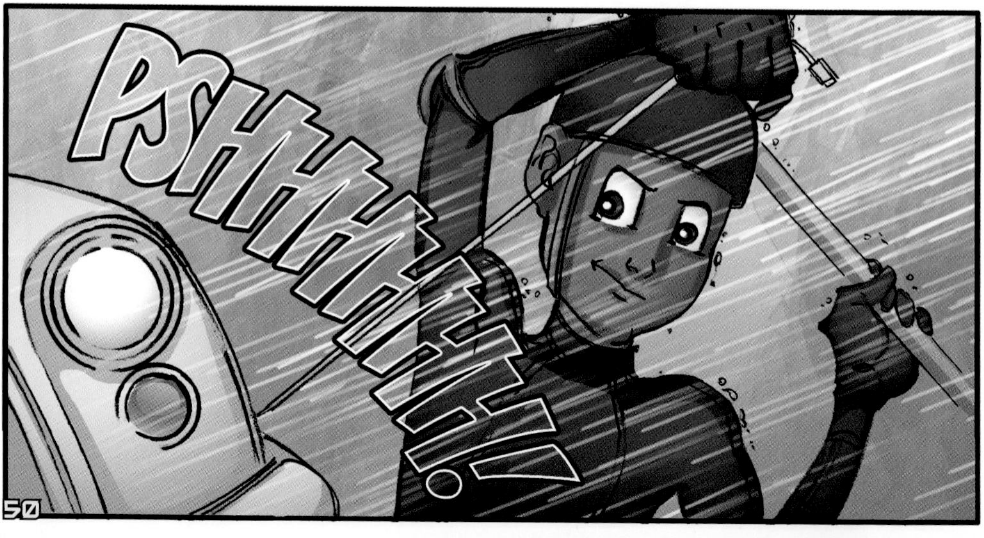
PSHHHHHH!!

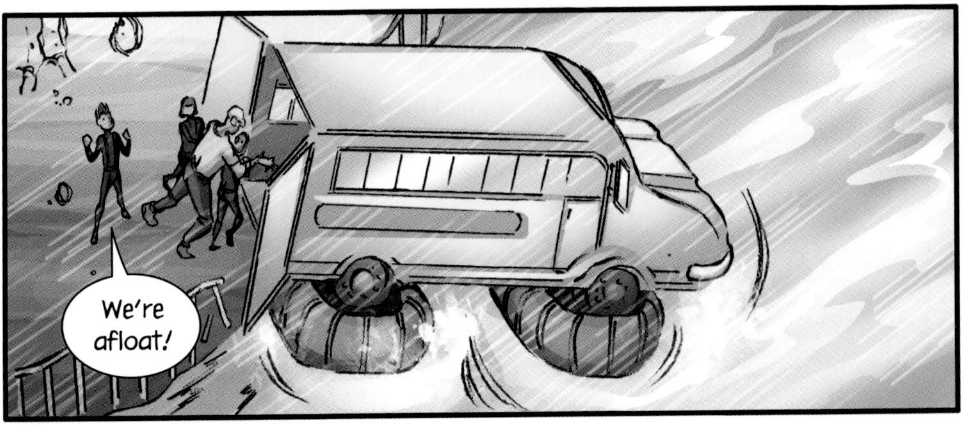
We're afloat!

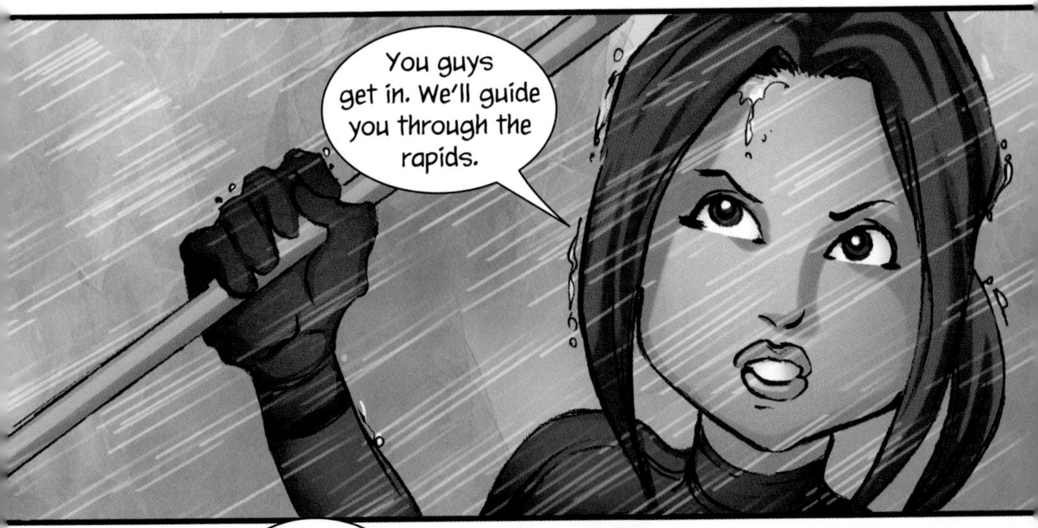
You guys get in. We'll guide you through the rapids.

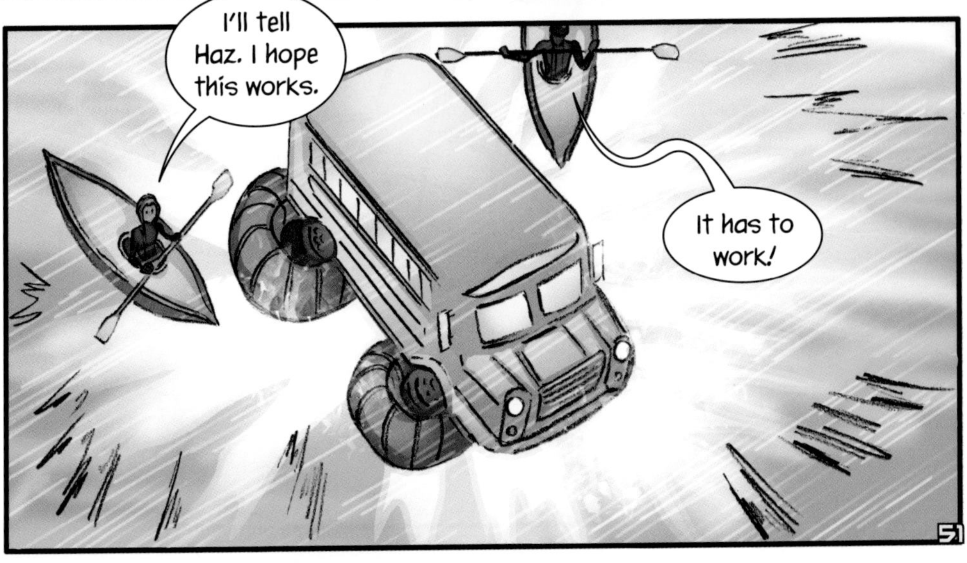
I'll tell Haz. I hope this works.
It has to work!

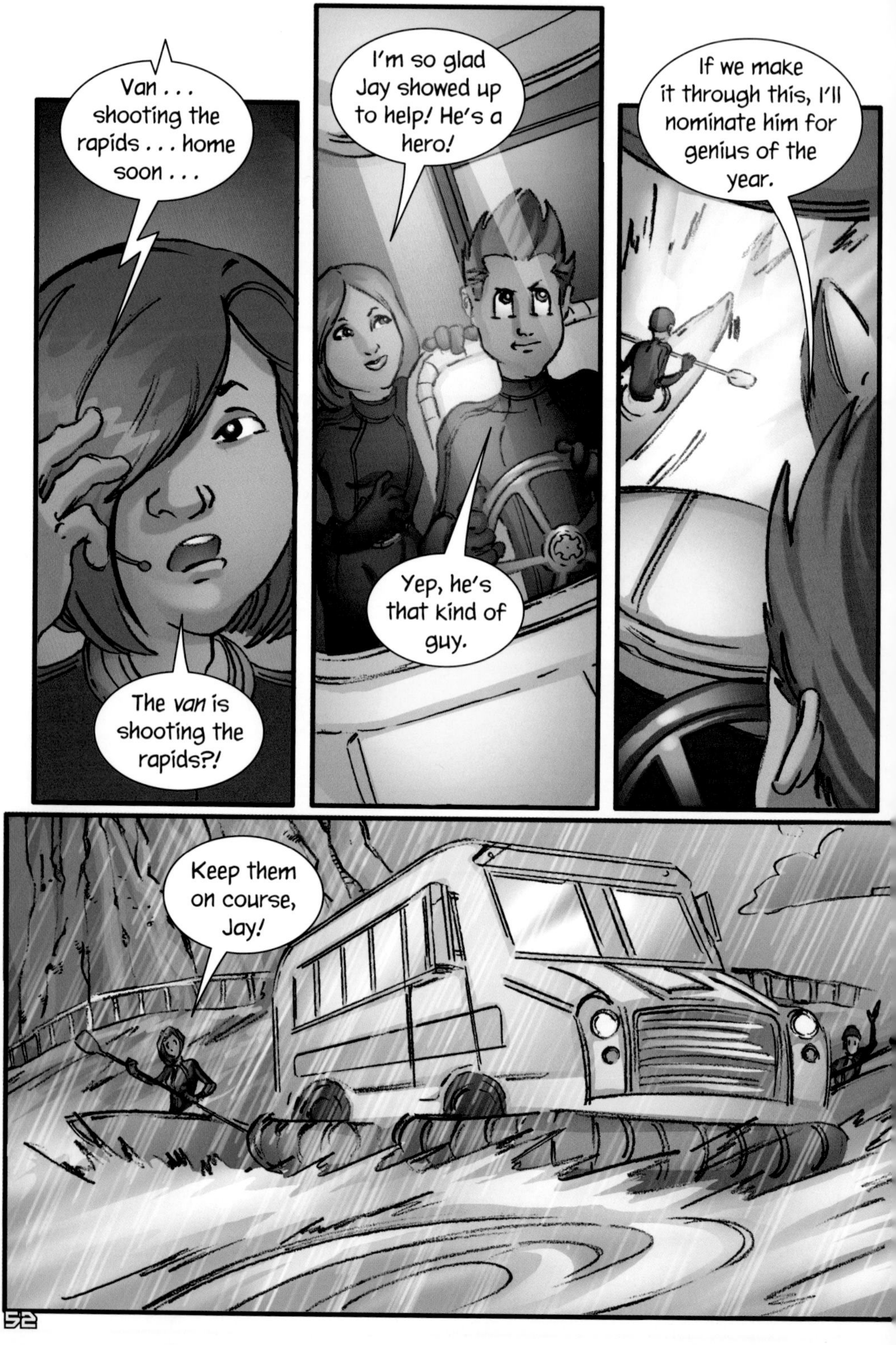
Van . . . shooting the rapids . . . home soon . . .
The *van* is shooting the rapids?!
I'm so glad Jay showed up to help! He's a hero!
Yep, he's that kind of guy.
If we make it through this, I'll nominate him for genius of the year.
Keep them on course, Jay!

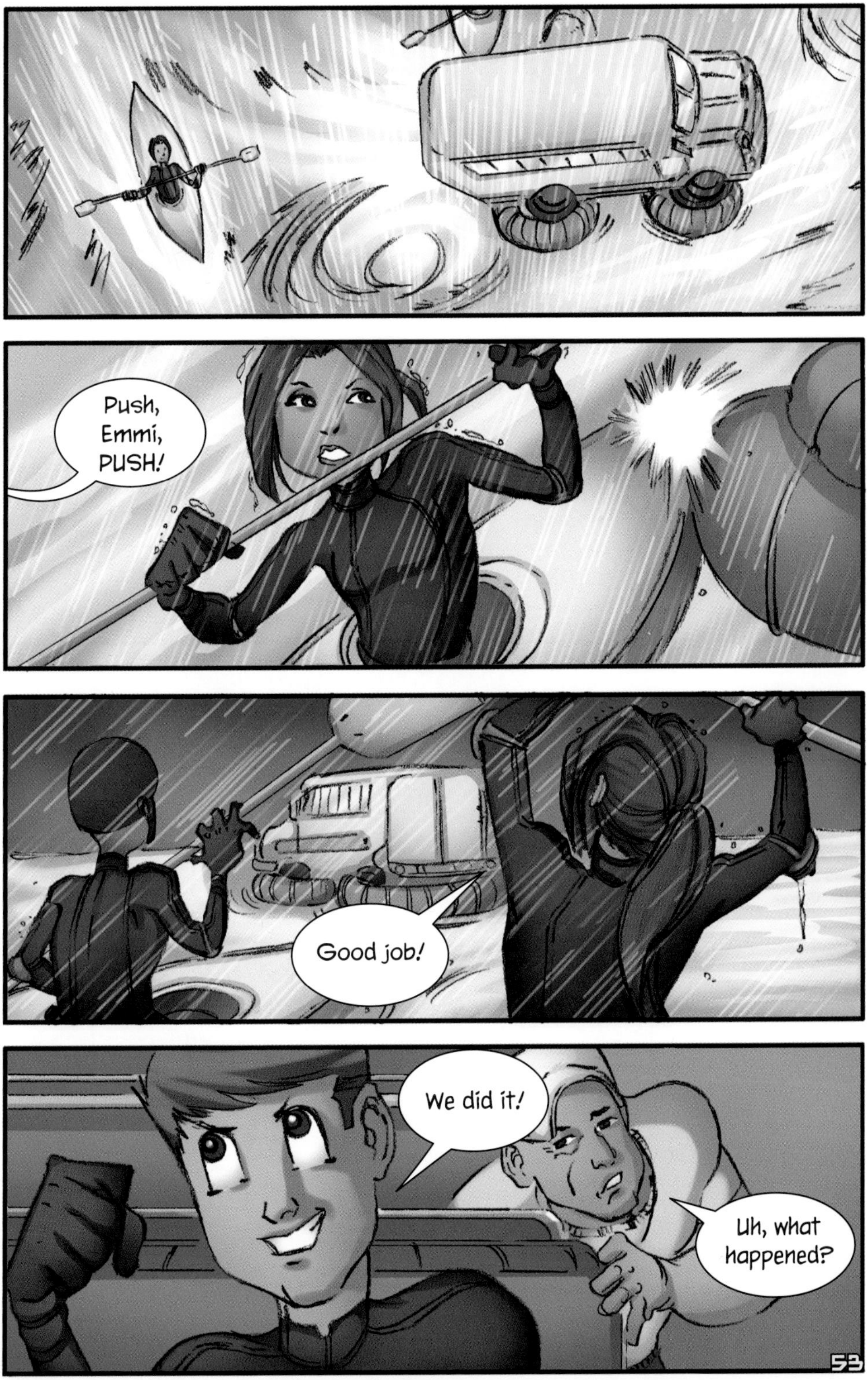
Push,
Emmi,
PUSH!
Good job!
We did it!
Uh, what
happened?

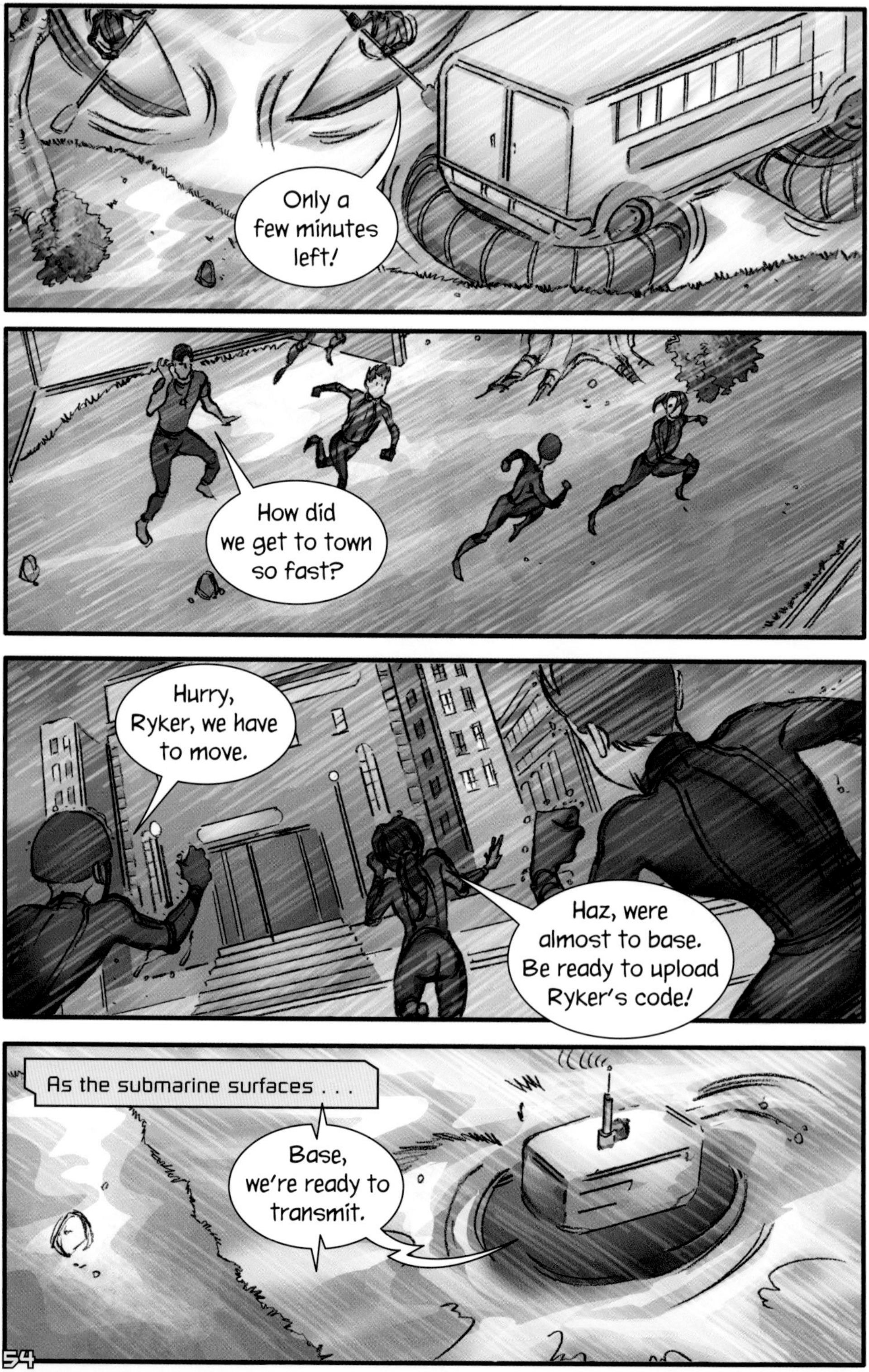
Only a few minutes left!
How did we get to town so fast?
Hurry, Ryker, we have to move.
Haz, were almost to base. Be ready to upload Ryker's code!
As the submarine surfaces . . .
Base, we're ready to transmit.

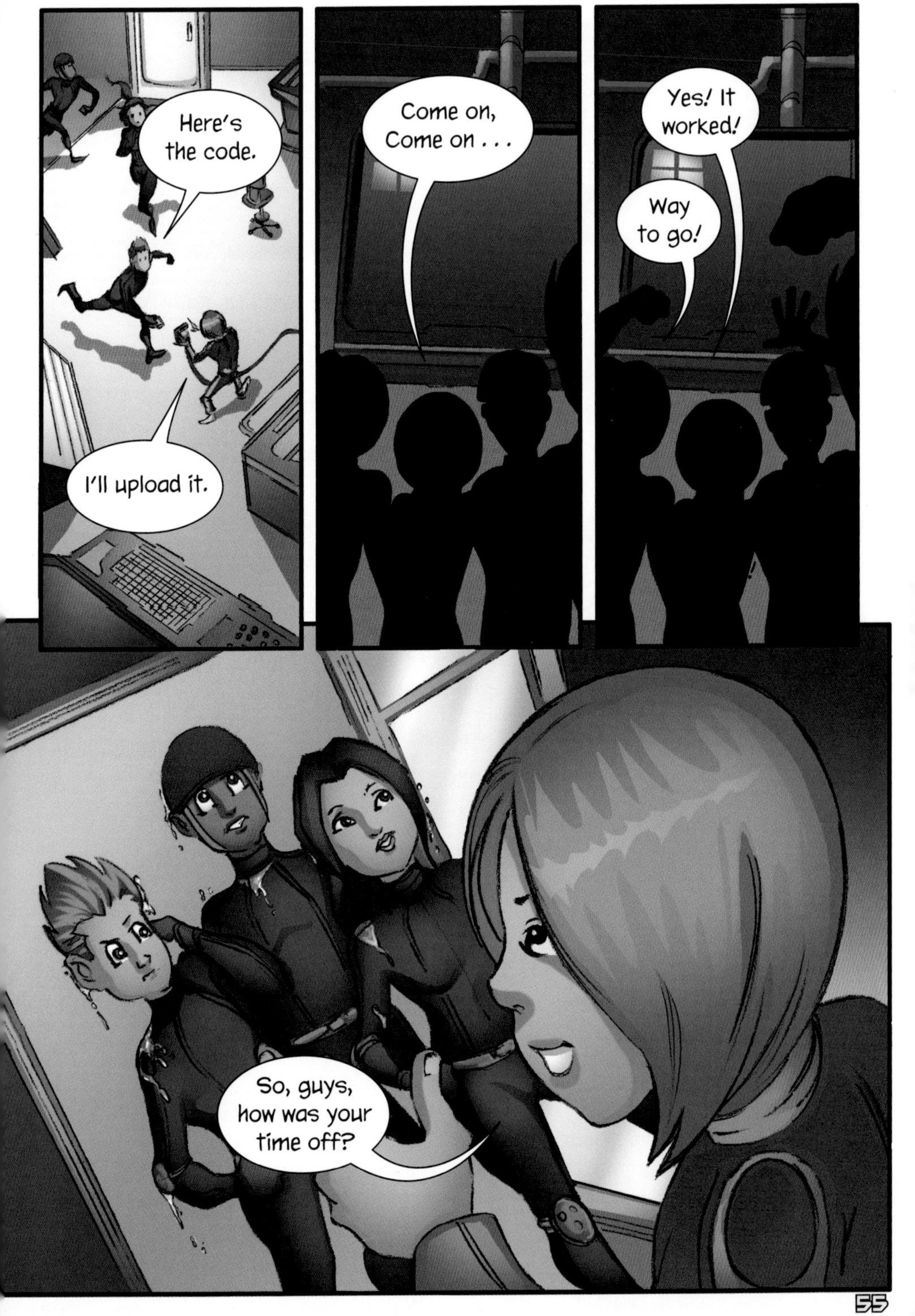
Here's the code.
I'll upload it.
Come on, Come on . . .
Yes! It worked!
Way to go!
So, guys, how was your time off?

SPYSPACE

a place for international spies

CHAT ROOM PROFILES

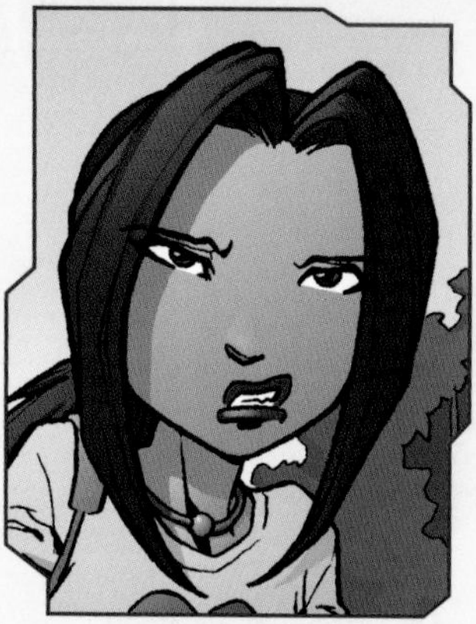

NAME: Emilia Rodriguez

AGE: 14

HEIGHT: 5' 3"

WEIGHT: 112 lbs.

EYES: Brown

HAIR: Brown

SPY ORG: Recon Academy

SPECIAL ABILITIES: Martial arts expert, gymnast, and all-around great athlete

NAME: Jeremiah Johnson

AGE: 13

HEIGHT: 5' 5"

WEIGHT: 120 lbs.

EYES: Brown

HAIR: None

SPY ORG: Recon Academy

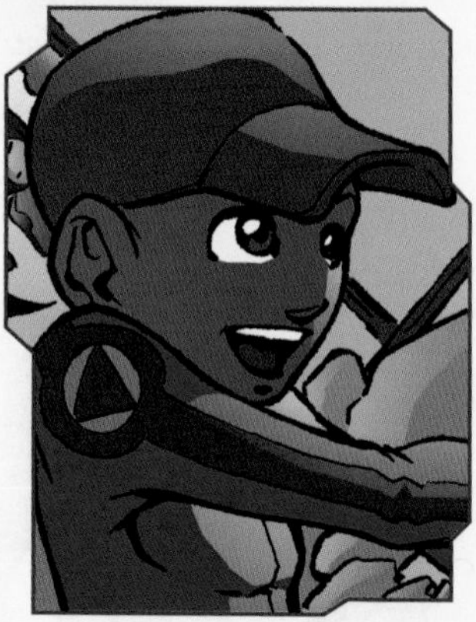

SPECIAL ABILITIES: Gadget guru and a totally gnarly skateboarder

HOME SEARCH BROWSE LOGOUT

PHOTOS

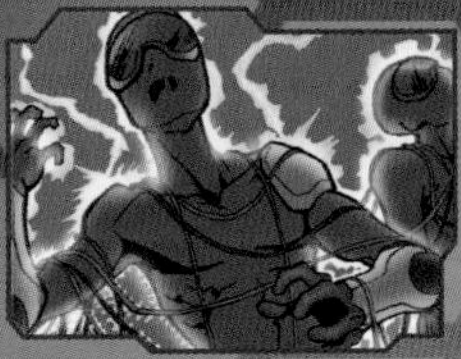
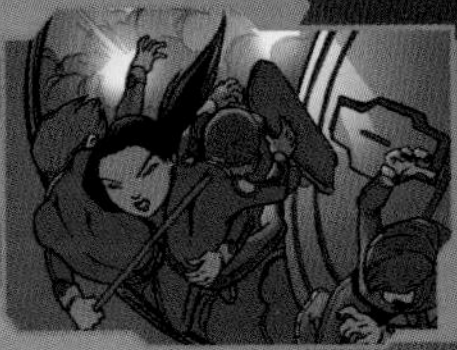
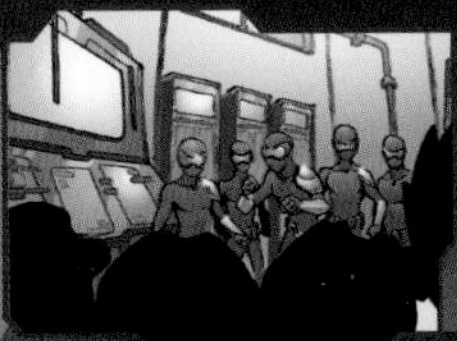

INSTANT CHAT

recent posts see all

Hi, Jay! It's sure good to be home, safe and sound. I still can't believe we made it down those rapids!!

Piece of cake, Emmi! It's no harder than climbing a mountain in the rain.

Yeah, if you're wearing rocket-fuel shoes!!

What do you have against my shoes? Rocket shoes are NOT cheating!

It's not the shoes, Jay. I just wish people could do things the old-fashioned way sometimes.

Oh yeah? Then maybe you should be writing me a letter instead of chatting online...

...Emmi, you still there?

Check your mailbox, Jay. You'll receive my answer in 3-5 business days.

› CASE FILE

CASE: "Storm Surge"
CASE NUMBER: 1434219186
AGENT: Emmi and Hazmat
ORGANIZATION: Recon Academy

SUBJECT:
Natural Disasters

OVERVIEW:
To maintain safety in Seaside, Recon Academy must keep their eyes on more than the city's evildoers. Recon must also keep their eyes to the skies, and prepare for all natural events.

POTENTIAL DANGERS:
- Hurricanes
- Floods
- Tornadoes
- Earthquakes
- Volcanoes
- Tsunamis

INTELLIGENCE:

active volcano (AK-tiv vol-KAY-no) — a mountain with vents through which lava, ash, and gas are capable of erupting

tsunami (soo-NAH-mee)—a very large, destructive wave often caused by an underwater earthquake

tornado alley (tor-NAY-doh AL-ee) — an area of the United States that includes South Dakota, Nebraska, Kansas, Oklahoma, northern Texas, and eastern Colorado, which experiences frequent tornadoes

INTRO:

Natural disasters can happen anywhere at anytime, destroying buildings and taking lives.

REGIONAL THREATS:

Gulf Coast — Hurricanes are the most dangerous threat to coastal zones. In fact, the deadliest U.S. natural disaster occurred on September 8, 1900, when a hurricane ripped through Galveston, Texas.

East Coast — Because of its highly populated cities, including New York, the East Coast of the United States is particularly vulnerable. Possible hurricanes and tsunamis could affect a large number of people.

West Coast — Besides hurricanes and tsunamis, Earthquakes also affect the western part of the United States. Scientists predict a megathrust earthquake could one day cause large-scale damage in California.

Midwest — Tornadoes pose the greatest threat to residents of the middle United States, especially in an area known as "Tornado Alley."

Mountains — More than 65 active volcanoes in the United States threaten residents of mountain regions.

CONCLUSION:

Preparedness is the best way to avoid significant impact from these unavoidable events.

› ABOUT THE AUTHOR

Chris Everheart always dreamed of interesting places, fascinating people, and exciting adventures. He is still a dreamer. He enjoys writing thrilling stories about young heroes who live in a world that doesn't always understand them. Chris lives in Tennessee with his family. He plans to travel to every continent on the globe, see interesting places, meet fascinating people, and have exciting adventures.

› ABOUT THE ILLUSTRATOR

Arcana Studios, Inc. was founded by Sean O'Reilly in Coquitlam, British Columbia, in 2004. Four years later, Arcana has established itself as Canada's largest comic book and graphic novel publisher with over 100 comics and 9 books released. A nomination for a Harvey Award and winning the Schuster Award for Top Publisher are just a few of Arcana's accolades. The studio is known as a quality publisher for independent comic books and graphic novels.

> GLOSSARY

antenna (an-TEN-uh)—a wire that receives radio and television signals

classified (KLASS-uh-fied)—declared secret by the government, as in "classified documents"

data (DAY-tuh)—information, or facts

decoding (dee-KODE-ing)—turning something that is written in code into ordinary language

deploy (di-PLOI)—to head out, or begin a mission

distress (diss-TRESS)—a feeling of great pain, sadness, or worry

satellite (SAT-uh-lite)—a spacecraft that orbits around Earth, which often transmits signals

secure (si-KYOOR)—make something safe, especially by guarding it

upload (UP-lohd)—to transfer data from one electronic device to another, such as from a memory card to a computer

› DISCUSSION QUESTIONS

1. In this book, Jay disobeys his coach and attempts to save Sarah on his own. Do you think this was a good idea? Why or why not?

2. When Ryker's cell phone breaks, he's unable to communicate with Hazmat. How would your life be different if you didn't have a phone? How would you communicate with friends and family?

3. Each Recon Academy member has a different talent and skill. What are some of your own talents and skills? How could your talents be used in the Recon Academy?

› WRITING PROMPTS

1. Write your own Recon Academy story. What type of problem will the team face? Which character will save the day and how? You decide.

2. Jay uses hi-tech gadgets to help get the job done. Write about a gadget you would like to have. How does it work? What types of things will it help you with?

3. Many graphic novels are written and illustrated by two different people. Write a story and then give it to a friend to illustrate. Remember, work together as a team.